The door flew i

Bolan followed in a rush, screen of cover fire, the stubby muzzle tracking in an arc from left to right across the room. The standing Nazi never had a chance to taste his beer as a string of parabellum hollowpoints ripped through his chest. His fellow Aryans were gaping at the black-clad stranger, stunned and speechless, when he blew them both away.

He checked the living room and found it empty, turning toward the stairs when he was challenged by a voice. This Nazi wore a pair of shorts and nothing else, but he was holding an automatic. As Bolan turned to face him, flame erupted from the muzzle.

One round whispered past his face as Bolan went to ground, a shoulder roll behind the nearest piece of furniture. Rounds two and three ripped through the easy chair that gave him cover, and he knew that he'd have to move or risk a hit with number four.

He came up firing, raked the staircase with a rising burst that caught the fascist waist-high. Momentum brought him down the stairs, and Bolan finished off the magazine before his target landed at the bottom.

He took a second to reload, then looked around.

Clean sweep.

MACK BOLAN®

The Executioner

#129 Haitian Hit	Stony Man Doctrine
#130 Dead Line	Terminal Velocity
#131 Ice Wolf	Resurrection Day
#132 The Big Kill	Dirty War
#133 Blood Run	Flight 741
#134 White Line War	Dead Easy
#135 Devil Force	Sudden Death
#136 Down and Dirty	Rogue Force
#137 Battle Lines	Tropic Heat
#138 Kill Trap	Fire in the Sky
#139 Cutting Edge	Anvil of Hell
#140 Wild Card	Flash Point
#141 Direct Hit	Flesh and Blood
#142 Fatal Error	Moving Target
#143 Helldust Cruise	Tightrope
#144 Whipsaw	Blowout
#145 Chicago Payoff	Blood Fever
#146 Deadly Tactics	Knockdown
#147 Payback Game	Assault
#148 Deep and Swift	Backlash
#149 Blood Rules	Siege
#150 Death Load	Blockade
#151 Message to Medellín	Evil Kingdom
#152 Combat Stretch	Counterblow
#153 Firebase Florida	Hardline
#154 Night Hit	Firepower
#155 Hawaiian Heat	Storm Burst
#156 Phantom Force	Intercept
#157 Cayman Strike	
#158 Firing Line	
#159 Steel and Flame	
#160 Storm Warning	
#161 Eye of the Storm	
#162 Colors of Hell	
#163 Warrior's Edge	
#164 Death Trail	
#165 Fire Sweep	

DON PENDLETON'S
THE EXECUTIONER®
FEATURING MACK BOLAN®

FIRE SWEEP

A GOLD EAGLE BOOK FROM
WORLDWIDE.

TORONTO • NEW YORK • LONDON
AMSTERDAM • PARIS • SYDNEY • HAMBURG
STOCKHOLM • ATHENS • TOKYO • MILAN
MADRID • WARSAW • BUDAPEST • AUCKLAND

First edition September 1992

ISBN 0-373-61165-X

Special thanks and acknowledgment to
Mike Newton for his contribution to this work.

FIRE SWEEP

Whenever a thing changes and quits its proper limits, this change is at once the death of that which was before.

—Lucretius

The world is changing every day, some changes for the better, some for the worse. Before those changes are complete, some things—some men—may have to die. So be it.

—Mack Bolan

To those responsible for finding peaceful solutions in the trouble spots of the world

PROLOGUE

It was nearly time.

Monica Jakes wondered yet again if the Russian was going to show. Granted, she'd arrived at the amusement park at least an hour before the meet, scoping out the terrain, imprinting escape routes on her mind in case the meet went sour.

And everything could go wrong, she reminded herself as nervous tension gnawed at the pit of her stomach. Then Monica relaxed, drawing comfort from the familiar feel of the Walther PPK beneath her lightweight jacket.

Her contact was a stranger, but she knew he'd be carrying a copy of *The New York Times* under one arm and wearing a carnation in his buttonhole. If he was anything like other Russians she'd known, the suit would barely fit and he'd have at least two chins.

She didn't know her contact's name, and her controller hadn't let her see a photograph. In case of any trouble, he'd explained, which *really* meant in case she was abducted and interrogated by the KGB.

It was enough to know she was meeting with a Russian double agent, valued for his contributions to the CIA. Most times, she reckoned, he must have another way of touching base with the Americans, but he was on vacation now, an overdue reward for sterling service to the Kremlin, and he'd selected Denmark for the rendezvous. With that decided it was only left to pick a tourist spot and make the contact a reality.

Which brought her back to here and now.

There was a certain irony, she thought, to meeting with another spy and swapping information that could get them killed while children ran and laughed around them, oblivious to any danger. Their own lives were a game of sorts, and you were never certain of the stakes until you threw the dice.

She spotted a carnation in the crowd, surprised to note the modern, well-cut suit. The paper folded underneath his arm could just as well have been *Der Spiegel,* but she took a chance and moved in his direction, taking care to keep it casual.

No double chins, she thought. In fact some women might consider him a handsome man, if they preferred the pale, ascetic type. Dark hair, cut short enough to leave his ears exposed, and he could use some sun.

Her eyes made fleeting contact with the Russian's, and she nodded toward a distant, unoccupied jungle gym. They were sixty feet apart but closing. In a few more moments . . .

The staccato sound of automatic gunfire made her flinch as a scream tore through the milling crowd. She saw her contact stumble and fling out his arms, the pages of his unread paper scattering as he fell.

And blood.

There was another blast, two weapons firing, and she spotted the gunners, dark men in leather jackets, open-collared shirts and blue jeans, firing Skorpions from the hip. They didn't seem to mind if one or two civilians joined their target on the ground.

She knew it was time to run, escape and save herself, but Monica stood fast. She palmed the Walther, flicking off the safety with her thumb, a live round waiting in the chamber as she took a firm two-handed grip and fired.

The nearest gunman staggered, the look of concentration on his face giving way to shock. She fired again and saw him fall, even as she swung her pistol toward the second target, waiting for a gray-haired man and several children to leave the line of fire.

Her adversary had no such compunction, squeezing off a short burst from his Skorpion that sent the old man sprawling. Monica dodged sideways, firing on the move, and knew that she'd missed the gunner as the pistol bucked against her palm. A wild shot was wasted on the crowd, and who knew where the bullet went. Incoming rounds whipped past her, pinging off the uprights of a metal swing set.

She flattened on the pavement, tourists dodging left and right, one hurdling her as she lined up another shot. Her enemy was beating a retreat, reloading on the run, lips moving as he muttered something to himself.

She needed luck to make the shot and got it, scoring with a hit behind the runner's knee. He twisted, falling on his backside, and squeezed off a burst that ripped through the air above her head. Behind her someone's scream was cut off in the middle of a rising note.

The Skorpion was small enough to fire one-handed, giving some mobility to Monica's opponent as he tried to scramble out of range. It wasn't easy, dragging one dead leg behind him, and he must have known he was finished when his second magazine ran dry. A clear shot now, and she'd never have a better chance.

Already up and moving, Monica fired once before she really got her balance, winging him. Then, again before she had a chance to brace and aim, she scored a lung shot on her second try, bringing crimson froth to the assassin's lips. Incredibly he tried to rise, blind fury and determination taking up where hope left off. Her last round drilled his forehead from a range of thirty feet and pitched him over backward, toppling him into a wading pool.

There was no time to waste. Someone must have called the police. She tucked her Walther out of sight and glanced back at her nameless contact, wondering what secrets had been stifled by a burst of automatic fire.

Too late.

The only way to salvage anything at all from the disaster was for her to slip away and file her own report as soon as possible. She could do nothing from a prison cell, and it would all have been in vain. Disgusted with herself, the secret agent turned and ran.

1

"I need a face-to-face, ASAP." Hal Brognola's voice was devoid of emotion over the phone, and a cold worm of anxiety began to wriggle in Mack Bolan's gut.

"Where?" Bolan asked.

"How's Indy sound? You haven't been there in a while, as I recall."

"Say when."

Brognola thought about it. Bolan pictured him behind his desk in Washington, consulting notes and clocks. "I need three hours minimum. Say half-past two and make it safe."

"That still leaves where."

"Let's do the Speedway, shall we? Open weekdays, there's a tour and a museum, whatever. Tourists in and out all the time."

"Too far for me to drive that fast," the Executioner replied.

"Forget the car. I'll make a call and have some transportation waiting for you at O'Hare. Pick up another rental when you land."

The line went dead, and Bolan frowned before he cradled the receiver. Any time Brognola called him off an active mission for a face-to-face, it meant some kind of emergency. Bad news, whatever it turned out to be.

No rush about O'Hare. Brognola would require a little time to make arrangements for the flight, and Bolan had to ditch his hardware first before he checked in with the rental car. He'd keep his side arm, just in case, and only ditch it if he had to check through at the gate for a commercial flight.

No word on how to find his contact at O'Hare, which meant the contact would be finding him. The key was staying on his toes, alert at every moment of the day and night. There was a simple rule for living on the edge: if you let your guard down, you died.

He took the rental back the way he'd come on Highway 94 and found the junction to O'Hare. No sweat so far.

But it would be much better, Bolan thought, if he had some idea of what was coming down. Before it landed on his head.

BROGNOLA'S SPOTTER waited for him near the rental car booth, a black man in a three-piece suit who looked uncomfortable with the cardboard placard reading Striker. Bolan closed the gap between them, nodded toward the sign and said, "That's me."

"Then, sir, you must know Leo's nickname from the old days."

"It was Pussy," Bolan answered, "but I wouldn't use it to his face."

The man looked relieved to fold his sign in two and drop it into the nearest trash can. "Follow me."

"I'll need to make a pit stop if we're checking through the gate."

"We won't be."

Fair enough. With his identity established by a password dating back to Bolan's early war against the Mafia, they moved along the teeming concourse, found an exit restricted to authorized personnel and made their way into the bowels of the terminal. Once they were off the main drag, Bolan's escort took credentials from an inside pocket of his coat and clipped them onto his lapel. He might not be the U.S. marshal the laminated card described, but he was close enough.

And he was packing heat.

The passing reference to Leo "The Pussy" Turrin brought back memories for Bolan, and he wondered how his old friend liked a desk in Washington these days. It was a long way from the front lines of the Boston Mob to liaison work at Justice, but if anyone could make the shift, it would be Leo.

Pussy? Bolan had to smile. Turrin wasn't even close.

A baby Lear was waiting on the tarmac, ready to depart. One thing about Brognola when he got his dander up, the big Fed didn't mess around. Perhaps three dozen government officials in the country had the power to reach out from a desk in Washington and make things happen in Chicago just like that. It was a measure of the man that Brognola didn't abuse his power in the slightest, or attempt to make his own life easier by pulling strings.

An honest man, no less. That made him part of an endangered species in the modern world, with numbers dropping all the time.

Inside the jet the warrior stowed his carryon and found himself a window seat. His escort wandered fore and aft, examining the head and then conferring with

the cockpit crew before he doubled back and sat across
the aisle.

"We estimate an hour's flight time once we get
clearance."

"Great."

What else was there to say? The marshal—if he *was*
a marshal—didn't welcome conversation. He was following specific orders to the letter, shuttling an unknown VIP between points A and B without a lot of
idle chitchat on the side. Nobody had to tell him it was
best for all concerned if he remained aloof and asked
no questions, meanwhile answering as few as possible.

They got their clearance moments later, and the Executioner would never know if it was luck or Brognola
at work behind the scenes. No matter, either way. The
Lear was comfortable, quiet, and his escort let the soldier rest in peace. He closed his eyes before they left the
ground and woke when they engaged the landing gear,
five minutes from touchdown at Indianapolis Inter-
national.

Going in, he had no bags to wait for, nothing to delay him as he followed the signs to reach another rental
car booth. His escort never left the plane, and Bolan
knew the man was glad to see him go. Another headache handed off to someone else before it soured and
became a killer migraine. One more face without a
name, another stranger to forget.

He used a "Michael Blanski" credit card to rent the
car for one day, with mileage on the house. The cute
brunette behind the counter let him have the map free,
and Bolan left to find his blue Corolla waiting in a
numbered space outside. His bag went into the back

seat, and he slid behind the wheel, remembering to buckle up for safety as he turned the key.

The dashboard digital said it was 12:15, which meant he had ample time to kill before his meeting with Brognola. Bolan motored north on Lynhurst Drive toward Speedway, something of a town within a city, named after the racetrack where the Indianapolis 500 was run each May. It was too early for a personal appearance at the track, and the warrior's stomach growled, reminding him that it had been eight hours since he'd made a breakfast out of hard-boiled eggs and water in Chicago. Time to refuel the machine.

He found a burger joint and went inside. A teenaged waitress took his order for a double burger, fries, some chili on the side and black coffee. It might not win a medal for nutrition, but he needed protein to remain alert and anything at all to keep his gut from snarling at him like a hungry animal.

Waiting for the second coming of his waitress, Bolan thought about the summons and Brognola's tone of voice. It was traditional to hold back the details, of course. You never really knew who might be listening in Washington, no matter if you scrambled calls and swept your phone lines every hour on the hour. There were ways to tap a line that didn't register on the machines, and who would be the wiser?

It was as paranoid as hell, but that was life in Washington since Watergate, the Iran-Contra affair and the rest of it. Brognola jokingly described the nation's capital as an asylum with the inmates in control, and Bolan sometimes wondered where the joke left off, reality intruding with a sick grin on its face. That kind of power was an aphrodisiac for some, a powerfully addictive drug for others. Few, once having tasted it, would give it up without a fight. In Washington the key to power—sometimes to survival—lay in knowledge. Who did what to whom and where.

Brognola did his job efficiently, successfully, and in a town like Washington, D.C., that meant he had to have enemies. When you were charged with taking major heavies off the street and putting them away for good, you had to figure on the heavies to resist. A wiretap here and there would be the least of it, and any time an operation leaked out in advance it meant a toll in wasted lives.

His food arrived, and Bolan was surprised to find it excellent. He cleaned his plate and had two refills of coffee as he waited, killing time. He still had forty minutes when he settled his bill and walked outside, but it was time to go.

Ten minutes to the track, with traffic, and he followed several other cars into a parking lot designed for larger crowds. Off-season thinned the herd, but there were always tourists who couldn't afford a ticket to the race itself, but were intent on seeing where the action all went down.

He bought a ticket, went inside and drifted toward the Racing Hall of Fame. Brognola might be here already, but he didn't like the odds. In any case, the Fed had opted not to specify a meeting point, and it would be his job to ferret Bolan out when he arrived. The last thing the Executioner needed was to advertise his presence at the track by hanging out around the entrance, looking like the victim of a blind date gone awry.

A group of Japanese were taking pictures while Bolan dawdled past the antique racing cars, slowly closing in on low-slung models of the present day. Technology had changed the sport so much in fifty years that early heroes of the track would feel like cavemen coming back today, surrounded by the flashy new machines that made their best times look as if they were standing still.

Times change.

But some things stay the same.

Bolan recognized Brognola's after-shave before he turned and found the big Fed watching him ten feet away.

"You getting psychic now?" Brognola asked as they shook hands.

"Old Spice. It never fails," the Executioner replied. "I hate to be predictable."

"The small things maybe. Shall we take a walk?"

"I thought you'd never ask."

Outside, they had more breathing room, less chance of being overheard. The afternoon was overcast but warm. If anybody gave the two of them a second glance, it didn't show.

"What's up?" Bolan asked.

"We've got an urgent problem overseas. You ever been to Norway?"

"Not that I recall."

"Nice country. Cool, this time of year, but nothing a jacket wouldn't fix."

"Let's start at the beginning, shall we?"

"Fair enough. Have you been keeping up with the news from Eastern Europe lately?"

"More or less. United Germany, free Poland, this and that. Red dominoes are falling for a change."

"You'd think so, anyway."

The Executioner said nothing, waiting for his friend to make a point. Hal didn't always blurt out what was on his mind, but he eventually got there if you gave him time.

"You won't be shocked to hear some people in the Kremlin aren't exactly thrilled to death with *perestroika*."

"So?"

"For them the recent changes are nothing to be proud of. It's a sellout of the dream from 1917, no less. Betrayal of the people's revolution by a gang of traitors. First the Eastern European satellites, and now they're chipping at the socialist republics one by one. We've got hard-liners looking for the first excuse they can find to put the brakes on *glasnost* here and now. They've got experience, material and motivation. Everything they need except the proper incident."

"That shouldn't be a problem," Bolan said.

"In fact, they may be working on it now."

"I'm listening."

"We've got a scientific conference coming up in Norway at a place called Lillehammer. It's down as East meets West, that kind of thing. Some dialogue, some party time. It's more for show than any actual exchange of information. If the first round works, we'll do the rest of it another time."

"It sounds routine."

"Would be except we've got ourselves a Czech physicist living in Moscow who's planning to defect."

"Is that still necessary?"

"Yes and no. Science is still a sensitive subject, especially physics. This guy has a lot of classified stuff in his head."

"You want this Czech to make it?"

"Me?" Brognola shrugged. "I wouldn't know his ass from Adam, if you want to know the truth. State wants him, though. He barely missed the Nobel prize in astrophysics two years running. Word is, he could really help out the space program if he agrees to play."

"And if he doesn't?"

"Great publicity for our side either way."

"So what's the problem? Bring him in."

"It's not that easy. We're hung up on a coincidence of sorts. State thinks somebody from the other side is working on a plan to scuttle *glasnost* with a vengeance sometime soon. The hard-liners have already tried it once. This time they might succeed. But there's another player in the game, too. There was supposed to be an information drop in Denmark, but it blew up in the agent's face. Three dead, one of them the contact. Interpol identified the other two as members of a German neo-Nazi clique, the Einsatzgruppe."

"That sounds familiar."

"It should," Brognola said, "if you've been brushing up on history. It's what the SS used to call their mobile killing squads. These bastards make no bones about their politics or what they have in mind for their opponents. On the books they're good for three known murders and at least a half-dozen bombings in the past twelve months."

"Nice guys."

"The best."

"One problem, though."

"Connections, right?"

"Affirmative. We've gone from a Czech defector to neo-Nazis raising hell in Denmark. What's the link?"

"Geography," Brognola replied. "Our Czech's supposed to make his move at the Lillehammer conference. According to the CIA, the best they could gather before their source was terminated, the Einsatzgruppe is looking at the same location for a major incident within the proper time frame."

"Ah."

"We don't know what they have in mind," Brognola went on, "but I gave up believing in coincidences some time ago."

"Smart move."

"The physicist's name is Gustave Lenart. We've got an agent on the ground in Norway, waiting to connect if you decide you want the job."

"Which job is that?"

"Security, I guess you'd say. State wants a watchdog for the transfer, but I'm more concerned about the neo-Nazi crowd and what they're working on. If worse comes to worst, I need somebody in the area who's good at pest control."

"How soon?"

"I can have you on a plane tonight."

"Did anybody ever tell you haste makes waste?"

"It rings a bell. The trouble is, the conference starts on Friday. More than half the delegates have already arrived, and Norway's working on a visit from their new king. He'll be giving them a pep talk over dinner, peace and understanding, this and that. It won't go over all that well with Hitler's grandkids shooting up the town."

"There's something missing," Bolan said.

"Such as."

"You started out with hard-line Communists, and now we're into neo-Nazis."

"So?"

"What happened to the Reds?"

"You're asking me?" Brognola shrugged. "I thought I might find out in your report."

"Terrific."

"That's the spirit. Any other questions?"

Too damn many, Bolan thought. For openers, he wondered why the CIA was bowing out of its traditional preserve—or was it? When Brognola said he had an agent on the ground, he wouldn't be referring to the personnel from Stony Man. That meant somebody from the Company, reporting back to Langley every time he made a move. And every time *Dolan* made a move.

It could be worse, of course. This way at least he recognized divided loyalties going in. They didn't have to dance around, pretending it was all for one and one for all. But if the spook from Langley tried to sell him out . . .

The Einsatzgruppe was another problem, complicating Bolan's job and multiplying the inherent risks. He was inclined to agree with Brognola on the coincidence factor, but where would the neo-Nazis strike if not at the scheduled scientific conference? Or was there yet another target in the Lillehammer area that Bolan knew nothing about?

One problem at a time. With a defector waiting in the wings he had to think about reactions from the Communists. In theory and on paper Moscow was loosening up and had no claims on a Czech national. Furthermore, the KGB had been put out of business . . . or had it? Was the present government entirely free of die-hard Reds? Were hard-line elements in Moscow so concerned about a certain Czech scientist that they'd try to reel him back if he escaped?

Again no answers came to mind. The Executioner would have to wait and see once he was on the ground in Norway and dealing with his ally and the opposition face-to-face.

In essence Brognola was asking him to root out the Einsatzgruppe and scotch their plans before they had a chance to realize a nightmare in the streets. If Bolan had a chance to baby-sit Gustave Lenart along the way, so much the better. And if they were right about the nonexistence of coincidence, those tasks might have a great deal more in common than it seemed.

Almost half a century had passed since Hitler put a pistol to his head and rang down the curtain on his Thousand Year Reich. In fact it had lasted only twelve years, but civilian casualties had averaged a million a year under Adolf's regime, and it would take at least another generation for Europeans to purge themselves of psychic pain and guilt. Such scars were slow to heal, and neo-Nazi terrorism would be doubly traumatic now, of all times, snapping at the heels of a fragile "new order" in Europe.

As for the left, could anyone *really* be certain what was happening behind the smiles and handshakes, all the affirmations of a brand-new Europe, free from domination by the Russian bear? Each time a Communist regime collapsed it left the newly ousted power brokers wondering what had happened, what had gone wrong. They had controlled the reins of life and death for decades, and losing power virtually overnight was bound to come as something of a shock. There would be some, no doubt, who still imagined they could play the same old games. And if the Kremlin tried to back them up...what then?

One problem at a time, Bolan thought. Don't bog down in needless worry. Words to live by in the hell-grounds where distractions from a troubled mind could spell disaster, even death.

"So what's the verdict?" Brognola asked. "Are you in?"

"I'm in."

2

The commercial flight from New York to Oslo took nine hours, and Bolan was relieved that he'd flown first-class, giving himself some breathing room. The human sardines back in economy would hit the ground with muscle cramps from head to toe and waste a day recovering from lack of sleep in transit while the Executioner was up for anything that came his way.

The immigration check at the airport was a formality, and Bolan's passport in the name of Michael Belasko got by without a second glance. For all intents and purposes he was a businessman on holiday, enjoying a diversion from the rat race. Only six or seven people in the world knew everything about his mission—Bolan's true identity, along with why he'd come to Norway. Even the CIA was in the dark concerning who Brognola had chosen to answer their request for help. If they ran checks on the Belasko cover—which they surely would—they'd find exactly what Brognola had had planted in the computers. The trail was cold, and barring leaks at Stony Man Farm should be impossible to trace.

As for his contact on the ground . . . well, trust was earned, not handed out like favors at a birthday party. He'd have to wait and see.

Bolan's bags came through with only superficial damage, and he passed the customs check with flying colors, moving toward the rental counter where he had a car reserved. The warrior had a gold credit card and a New York driver's license in the Belasko name, in addition to his passport, and the paperwork was minimal. After acquiring some more maps to help him find his way, Bolan left the airport in a new VW two-door for the fifteen-minute drive to Oslo proper.

On paper Oslo was the tenth-largest city in the world for total area, but the statistic was largely a bureaucratic convenience. In fact the built-up area was small by comparison with Stockholm and Copenhagen, much less the regional giants of London, Paris and Rome. More famous for its harbor and surrounding mountains than its architecture, Oslo was a hospitable, if somewhat low-key, capital city, but it played no part in Bolan's plans.

His goal was Lillehammer, a hundred miles due north along the western tip of Lake Mjosa. He had open highway start to finish, making decent time and winking at the posted limits in the absence of police. Around him there was fertile farmland interspersed with forest underneath the bluest sky the Executioner had ever seen. He passed a paddle steamer on the lake, and nearing Hamar, Bolan had a glimpse of Helgoy—Saints' Island—where leading Norwegian clergymen were interned for anti-Nazi activities during the Second World War.

He tried to picture the reaction of the locals to the modern Einsatzgruppe, based on recent history, and he kept coming up with lynch mobs, farmers waving pitchforks in the air and dishing out rough justice to the brownshirts on their own.

It might be worth a look, but it would certainly result in innocent civilians being killed or injured. Given any kind of chance at all, he hoped to keep the game between professionals...and give the fledgling fascists something to remember on his own. A little taste of Bolan went a long, long way among the savages.

Approaching Lillehammer through the scenic valley of Gubrandsdal, Bolan checked his rearview mirror periodically to make sure he hadn't acquired a tail along the way. It seemed unlikely, but his dealings with the CIA on other missions had prepared him for duplicity at every turn. And if the Company was working Lillehammer, then it stood to reason that its competition from the East wouldn't be far behind.

His cover should be solid so far, but the very fact of his arrival could be enough to alert the enemy. The KGB had no more faith in coincidence than Bolan did, and he couldn't ignore the possibility of watchers following his every public move, cover or not.

It was the private moves, however, that would get him where he had to go.

Lillehammer was a cultural and tourist center, best known as the home of author and Nobel prize winner Sigrid Undset. Violence was a negligible factor in the postwar years, but that could change dramatically as outside forces sought to use the peaceful city for a chessboard, scheming toward their separate, selfish ends.

The stage was set for unaccustomed bloodshed, and the Executioner wasn't convinced he could head it off entirely. With a little luck, however, he might still be able to confine the mayhem, making sure those responsible for any violence paid their rightful dues.

His room was waiting at the Oppland hotel, third-floor accommodations with a private bath. The porter took his bags while Bolan signed the register and got his key.

The room was small but spotless with a fair view of the lake. He tipped the porter, saw him out and stood before the window for a moment, checking out the panoramic view. There was a feel of history about the town, despite its modern structures interspersed among the old, and with the mountains close at hand he understood the standard Norseman's love of outdoor sports. He caught himself translating altitude and angles into rifle shots, assessing difficulty, and he pushed the morbid thoughts away.

Not yet.

Unless he missed his guess the violence would be coming soon enough.

First-class or not, the flight and drive had taken something out of him, and he was moving toward the shower when a rapping on the door distracted him.

The open door revealed a honey blonde, five seven, with a trim, athletic build. Her eyes were emerald green and cautious as she looked him over, taking stock of Bolan in her mind. A smallish suitcase stood beside her on the floor.

"Mr. Belasko?"

"Yes?"

"The last piece of your luggage, sir. I must apologize for the delay."

"It's here now," Bolan said, responding to the password. "That's the only thing that counts."

"May I come in?"

"Of course."

He stood aside and let her bring the suitcase with her, waiting while she dropped it on the bed. She raised one hand and swirled her index finger in a circuit of the room, her eyebrows lifted in a question.

Bolan shook his head. He didn't have the gear to check the room for microphones.

Without another word his contact opened the bag and lifted out a small transistor radio, extending the antenna as she switched it on. He watched her move around the room with static hissing from the radio, a point between established channels, waiting for the squawk of feedback that would indicate a bug in place. When she checked out the sleeping room and bathroom without a hit, she killed the radio and left it on the dresser.

"There."

"You made good time," he commented.

"I'm staying here in the hotel."

"Convenient."

Bolan might have missed the accent, if he hadn't known her background. Native Czech, an exile in the days before the walls had come down. According to Brognola's briefing, she'd been recruited by the CIA because of expertise on Eastern Bloc activities. Politically she'd been branded a rebel in her native land, required to flee or face imprisonment for opposition to the state. Her name and photograph hadn't been included in the brief.

"What else is in the bag?" he asked.

"I did my best with what we had available. There wasn't that much time."

"Okay."

The pistol was a new Beretta 92-F semiautomatic, with the muzzle threaded to accommodate a silencer that had its own slot in the bag. He counted a half-dozen extra magazines, with spare 9 mm rounds in boxes filling up a corner of the case. A Heckler & Koch MP-5K submachine gun was secured in place by Velcro straps, curved magazines packed in around it. The sampling of grenades included high-explosive, frag, incendiary and concussion.

"Not bad for short notice."

"We aim to please."

"The Langley motto?"

"More or less."

"Why don't we talk about the job?"

"Yes, please."

"But first, I need a name."

"Excuse me?"

"Yours."

The smile broke through in spite of her. "It's Monica. Monica Jakes."

Or maybe not, but Bolan wasn't overly concerned about the name. In any case, it beat "Hey, you."

"Please, have a seat."

She nodded, took the only chair and left him with the bed.

"You're set to make the transfer with Lenart?" Bolan asked.

"That's right."

"What kind of schedule are we looking at?"

"The conference starts tomorrow, running through the weekend. He could make the move anytime."

"You're ready for a lift?"

"We're covering the options," she informed him, "any way it goes."

"Except you've hit a snag, I understand."

"We have," she said with obvious reluctance.

"So?"

"How much have you been told?"

"The basics."

There was silence for another moment as she finished taking stock of Bolan, wondering how much detail it would be safe to tell him about her mission. Finally she seemed to make up her mind and leaned forward slightly in her chair.

"You know about Gustave Lenart," she said. "At first my job was limited to making sure he got across without a problem. Then, about three weeks ago, came word from one of Langley's double agents in the KGB about a 'special project' in the area, designed to coincide with the assembly."

"Any details?"

"No. A warning only. It was said to be too sensitive for regular transmission channels, so a meeting was arranged on neutral ground. Our contact was supposed to fill me in, but he was killed before we had a chance to speak."

"And now the shooters have been traced back to the Einsatzgruppe."

"Yes."

"It doesn't fit," Bolan said. "How would members of a German neo-Nazi gang find out about your meeting? Come to that, why should they care?"

"You know the answer to your first question—they were informed by someone who had knowledge of the meeting place and time. As for the second part...what do you know about the Einsatzgruppe?''

"They come off like a right-wing version of the Baader-Meinhof gang," he answered. "Swastikas and slogans in the early days before they made the move to terrorism. Estimated hard-core membership approximately twenty-five. Say twice that many hangers-on, a few contributors who keep the party rolling in between bank robberies and kidnappings.''

"There's more," his contact said. "Our information shows the Einsatzgruppe involved itself in several contract murders in the past six months. It seems their politics can take a back seat if the price is right."

"You think they tagged your Russian on a contract?''

"We've considered it. The other option would suggest direct involvement by the Einsatzgruppe in the incident prepared by certain elements in Moscow.''

"Sort of like another nonaggression pact?''

"In essence. The Soviet hard-liners pay the bills while neo-Nazis pull the triggers, plant the bombs... whatever. If arrests are made, the Einsatzgruppe stands alone.''

"Unless they talk.''

"And tell their fascist friends they were really working for Soviets?'' She smiled and shook her head. "I don't think so.''

"Okay, it works for me. Two problems, though.''

"Just two?''

"So far. I can't do anything about the Einsatzgruppe until we find out where they are. And while we're at it, it would be a major help to know exactly what the Russians have in mind.''

"I'm working on the first part," Monica replied. "They can't be far away if they intend to strike this weekend. As soon as I hear anything at all, I'll let you know."

"And what about the second part?"

"More difficult. The killing broke our contact with the KGB. I can't help thinking that their strike must be related to the conference, from the timing and location. If they simply wanted tourists, they could find a site with larger crowds and move at any time."

"The conference, then. I'm told it's basically a show of friendship more than anything."

"Correct. If all goes well, the real exchange of information will be carried out at future meetings."

"If it fails?"

"The spirit of cooperation would be jeopardized, of course. Beyond that, if the neo-Nazis were involved, there'd be repercussions felt throughout the continent. Old wounds are slow to heal, and with a newly reunited Germany..."

She let the sentence trail away, but Bolan knew where she was going. He'd talked about the same thing with Brognola, and the problem had been in his mind throughout the flight from JFK. If there was any one thing calculated to divert attention from the Soviet Union and cause a European panic, it would be the specter of a Fourth Reich rising to assert itself. A Nazi renaissance would set off tremors from Berlin to Tel Aviv, reviving images of death camps, crematoriums and Panzer columns trailing mass destruction in their wake. The fear alone might be enough to raise demands for occupation or a new division of the German state, and Moscow wouldn't have to hit the panic button first. The Czechs and Poles, the Dutch and French, the Finns and British—all these and more had cause to dread a second coming of the swastika in Europe.

It could work, he realized, but they'd need the proper target. Taking out a group of scientists whose names were rarely heard outside of academic circles in their native countries would provoke some outcry, granted, but unless they tried to string out a hostage situation for days or weeks, it didn't qualify for great publicity. The Einsatzgruppe needed something more spectacular to guarantee an audience. A king, for instance.

"I was told King Harald will be speaking at the conference," Bolan said.

"Yes. They have a formal dinner Friday night to open the proceedings. He's supposed to make a speech and welcome the participants, that sort of thing."

"Sounds like the kind of target a Nazi might appreciate."

"You might be right."

"He'll have security, of course, but I'd feel better if the Einsatzgruppe was neutralized beforehand."

"How?"

"That's my job," the Executioner said grimly. "Yours is finding out where I can reach them sometime prior to Friday night."

It gave her two days, give or take, but Monica didn't recoil in shock. She merely nodded, frowned and said, "I'll do my best."

"Until then . . ."

"You'll be here in case I need to reach you?"

"More or less. We'll need to keep in touch."

"A waiting game," she said.

"The trick is filling up your time so you don't mind the wait."

"Perhaps if you would join me later in the dining room...?"

"Say eight o'clock?"

"I'll see you then."

She left, and Bolan double-locked the door behind her, as he sorted through the puzzle pieces in his mind. They had the working outline of a devious conspiracy, but there were gaping holes where major players ought to be. A clean sweep needed firm intelligence, and Bolan wasn't even close.

Not yet.

He sat on the bed and started fieldstripping his weapons, checking out extractors, firing pins and cartridges, the springs in magazines. There was no point in leaving anything to chance.

The lady was a knockout, but he made a point of trusting no one with his life on short acquaintance. She'd have to earn that trust, like everybody else, and she could start by pinning down the Einsatzgruppe for a swift preemptive strike.

He'd feel better when the neo-Nazis had been neutralized. That done, the transfer of Lenart should be a relatively simple task.

Should be. How many times had those two words blown up in Bolan's face? Too many, right?

The world *should be* a better place, but he was stuck with grim reality from day to day, and he'd work with what he had one problem at a time until he solved them all or one turned out to be insolvable.

In which case he was dead.

But if it went that way, the Executioner wouldn't be going down alone.

3

The Victoria hotel in Hamar stood at 21 Strandgaten, its westward-facing rooms providing a magnificent view of Lake Mjosa at its widest point, Saints' Island bristling with trees across the water. It wasn't the view, however, that commanded Otto Thadden's full attention as he left his gray Mercedes in the car park, taking time to set the tamper-proof alarm before he circled toward the hotel entrance.

Thadden was concerned with windows at the moment. There were far too many of them for his liking, and he knew from personal experience that any one could hide a spotter with field glasses, a telephoto camera or directional microphone. While he was at it he couldn't rule out the possibility of snipers. Thadden was a relatively honest man, at least in terms of self-evaluation, and he knew there were countless individuals who wished him dead.

But they weren't about to get their wish today.

He reached the hotel lobby and paused to sweep the room in search of a familiar face. There should be none, but you could never tell. A little paranoia was the surest form of life insurance when you worked in the intelligence community.

Of course, Thadden was "retired" now. He had been unemployed, officially, since the reunion of divided Germany had become an established fact. As a commander of the East German secret police, his services were no longer welcome, his allegiance to the goals of global communism a decided liability. It hardly mattered, since the liberal idiots in Moscow had decided there was no such thing as global communism anymore, but Germans had long memories. The work he had done was widely misinterpreted today, his former government reviled by peasants anxious for a chance to act American. Ten minutes in the basement of the old headquarters building in East Berlin and they would sing a different tune, he thought grimly.

Unlike a number of his comrades, Thadden had been wise enough to see the end approaching. Some of his associates had stubbornly refused to brace themselves for a collision with reality, denying such reactionary change was possible despite the evidence. A few of them had been despondent to the point of suicide, while others had fled to Russia, seeking sanctuary with the idiots who had abandoned them.

A little preparation had saved the day for Otto Thadden. Even die-hard Communists had to plan ahead, and one of Thadden's plans had included Switzerland, where accumulated payoffs had been drawing interest in a safe account for years. He had earned a lot of money squeezing his black-market contacts, pimps, whores and the odd narcotics dealer—even more letting dissidents procure a little comfort for a price. When it was time to leave, he'd had a tidy nest egg waiting for him in the shadow of the Alps, and he was reasonably certain he wouldn't be forced to work again.

But it wasn't enough. Security was one thing, and fulfillment something else again. For Otto Thadden there would be no peace of mind until he had repaid the insults suffered in the recent past when everything he believed in, all he had worked for in his life, had been swept away by anarchists and rabble.

It was time to turn the game around, and Thadden was prepared to do his part. It helped that certain people in Moscow would be putting up the money and providing all the necessary hardware, though he could have made a decent contribution on his own. The basic plan was feasible, although he questioned whether anyone could now undo the damage of reunion, but it might not be too late to stem the tide in Eastern Europe.

First, however, there would have to be some changes made.

When he was satisfied no one in the hotel lobby seemed to be a spy, he moved in the direction of the elevators. Waiting for the car, he stood partially turned toward the lobby, conscious of the Browning automatic pistol slung beneath his arm in quick-draw leather. He'd rather not spill blood in public, if the incident could be avoided, but he had no moral qualms about another death.

What did it matter, one corpse more or less? Provided, always, the corpse wasn't his own.

He had the elevator to himself, and no one saw him exit on the seventh floor. He moved along the hallway like a stalking panther, one hand underneath his jacket now, ready with the gun in case a door should suddenly fly open to reveal an enemy. In other circumstances Thadden might have felt ridiculous, but he had come too far and risked too much to make-believe he wasn't in danger now. They all had enemies, and every day that moved them closer to the execution of their master plan increased the mortal risk involved.

Room 705 was silent as he approached, no sound of conversation from behind the door. He checked his watch and found he was forty seconds early. Still, he shouldn't be the first. Svoboda always turned up well ahead of time, as if he thought the others would begin without him. As for Rostov...

Thadden hoped there would be progress to report this time. Their last two meetings had been brief and nearly pointless, simple confirmations of the game plan still on track. A phone call could have done the job, except that they were all afraid of open lines these days.

With reason.

Life had taught him there were spies and traitors everywhere. The ties of blood weren't enough to guarantee fidelity, much less the bland espousal of a creed or doctrine. Thadden trusted no one but himself, but he could work with others if their goals appeared to coincide. Beyond that point each person was expendable.

It helped to know that Rostov and Svoboda felt the same. He understood such men and knew they'd sacrifice each other if it came to that. They made no hollow claims of friendship or fidelity beyond their mission of the moment, which had drawn them together here and now.

He knocked and waited and was about to try again when footsteps sounded on the far side of the door. A latch was disengaged, and in another moment he was staring as Svoboda's face.

"You're late," the Czech informed him.

"No, your watch is fast. As usual."

"Come in." It was the Russian's voice, serene and unmistakable.

He heard Svoboda lock the door behind him, spared a nod for Rostov and deliberately sat in what he took to be Svoboda's chair. The Czech regarded him with vague disdain and found another seat.

The Russian favored both of them with a laconic smile and said, "Shall we begin?"

EDUARD SVOBODA HATED waiting most of all. It seemed that he'd spent a lifetime waiting—for his parents, for superiors and later for subordinates to finish their appointed tasks. Since cursed "freedom" had come to Prague, he'd been waiting for an opportunity to reassert himself and take back what was rightly his.

Position. Influence. The awe of lesser men.

Before the Soviets had given up on Czechoslovakia Svoboda had been a ranking officer in the Statni Tajna Bezpenost—State Secret Security—working closely with the KGB to fight subversion in his native land. His specialty had been interrogations, yet another kind of waiting game, but one in which he had a talent for manipulating time. If he desired an answer, it would come. The choice was his to reach a quick solution or prolong the moment for his own enjoyment and the education of his staff.

The past four months he had been working overtime to win the power back. A few more days . . .

"Shall we begin?"

The Russian, Rostov, never raised his voice. Instead, if he grew angry or impatient, he spoke more softly, forcing those around him to lean closer and strain their ears for every word. It was a clever tactic of manipulation, coupled with the way his eyes turned as cold and hard as flint when he was driving home a special point.

They were killer's eyes, Svoboda thought...but then all of them were killers here.

"What progress?" Thadden asked, directing his comment to no one in particular.

"Our leak had been disposed of," Rostov said. In place of pride he seemed embarrassed that the matter had come up at all.

The German frowned. "Who was it?"

"Dmitri Kolov from the Seventh Directorate," Rostov replied. "Surveillance work. God knows how long he was selling information to the West."

It was ironic, Svoboda thought, for a die-hard Communist and colonel in the KGB to use the name of God in vain or otherwise. Perhaps it was a reflex, or a private joke. "He knew about our plans?" the Czech inquired.

"Impossible to say. I verified his interest in the Einsatzgruppe and ordered termination automatically. It may have been another routine information drop, but we should all assume the worst."

"Which means?" The frown on Thadden's face carved furrows in his cheeks.

"The possibility of some exposure," Rostov answered. "Kolov didn't have a chance to speak with anyone before he died. That much we know. As for his previous disclosures, well . . ."

The silence said it all. They were at risk, but danger had been part of their design from the beginning. All of them had gone too far to scuttle now, assuming they could withdraw at all.

"It was a good thing," Svoboda said, "using Norner's people."

"He was angered by the loss, of course," Rostov said, "but some cash will put that right. He still has ample numbers for the job at hand."

"And afterward?" Thadden asked.

"Fascists come and go," Rostov replied. "There are always more available if we require their services."

"Suppose they manage to escape?" Svoboda asked.

"So much the better." Rostov's smile was predatory. "Nazis on a rampage, terrorizing Scandinavia. The longer they remain at large, the more we reap in terms of propaganda."

"And if some of them are captured still alive?"

"A show trial. More publicity. We should be grateful."

"They may talk."

"And implicate themselves in yet another killing? I don't think so. If they wish to boast about contributors, so be it. Our donations to the cause have all been routed through a dummy corporation in Geneva, as agreed. The trail ends there, if anybody chases it that far."

"I understand you met with Koch and Norner, though," Svoboda challenged.

"True, on one occasion. Naturally I didn't introduce myself by name. Let the police trot out their mug books with the photographs of wealthy fascists and decrepit SS veterans. Who cares?"

"We're covered then." There was a measure of relief in Thadden's voice.

"Of course."

"Unless your leak, this Kolov, has informed his contacts in the West."

"The conference is proceeding in accordance with the schedule," Rostov said. "The king will make his speech on Friday night as planned. And there's one more bonus."

"Ah?"

"One of the physicists, a Czech—" the colonel nodded at Svoboda as he spoke "—is planning to defect."

"What relevance—" Thadden began.

"A sideshow possibly. Or one more victim of the fascist Einsatzgruppe. Why not let the baby Hitlers do our dirty work . . . and take the blame?"

"The documents?" Svoboda asked.

"All ready."

"And the mailing?"

"Prearranged," Rostov said, keeping up his plastic smile.

Rostov's group in the KGB had made arrangements for the mailing of communiqués, purportedly authored by leaders of the Einsatzgruppe, claiming credit for the incident they had in mind. It struck Svoboda that the neo-Nazis probably would boast about it on their own, but circumstances might prohibit them from making contact with the press. If most or all of them were killed, for instance, then the papers forged by Rostov's people would be mailed, regardless. The only hitch would be if Norner's people failed in their attempt and a communiqué announcing their success was issued by mistake.

"You've used a fail-safe system just in case?" Svoboda asked.

"You mean in case of failure?" Rostov pinned the Czech with his flinty eyes. "Of course. We aren't amateurs."

"I meant no insult, Comrade."

"None was taken . . . *Comrade*."

Rostov's condescending tone was typical. Most Russians thought that Moscow was the center of the universe, and they were prone to treat their foreign allies with a corresponding disrespect, no matter how much the country was deteriorating. Still, Rostov was the man with the plan and the money. His vote was final, and he hadn't failed them yet. And if he did, what then?

Svoboda's fifteen years of service with the STB in Prague had taught him the importance of a fallback option. Plausible deniability. Escape. Self-preservation in a pinch. He trusted Rostov's judgment to a point, but he wasn't about to sacrifice himself for any man— or any cause. If things went badly in the next few days, he was prepared to disappear and let the others sort it out.

Was there a place on earth where he could hide from Rostov and his KGB henchmen? Perhaps.

"The Einsatzgruppe is in place?" Thadden asked.

"Yes," Rostov replied. "Their men are only waiting for the proper time."

"So close," the German said.

"And if they fail?" Svoboda asked.

The Russian lost his smile. "The mere attempt should be enough, but I've left nothing to chance. Another fail-safe option, as you say."

"Which is?" Svoboda asked.

"My secret," Rostov replied. "The details don't concern you now."

The Czech glanced at Thadden and caught the German scowling, but he held his tongue. It might be best this time to let the colonel play his games alone. That way, if Rostov's secret gambit blew up in his face, there would be nothing to connect Svoboda with the plot. "We're ready, then," he stated.

"As ready as we'll ever be," Thadden said.

"No more questions?" Rostov asked.

Svoboda shook his head, already rising from his chair. The less time spent in Rostov's company from this point on, the safer he would be.

"In that case I shall speak to you on Friday night," the Russian said. "When I have good news to report."

"Until then, Comrade," Svoboda said.

"Until then."

Outside, retreating toward the elevator, Thadden turned to his companion. "He's cool, that Russian."

"Yes."

"Too cool perhaps."

"You think there may be problems?"

"We shall see."

"And if there are?" Svoboda prodded, feeling anxious now.

"Then someone has to clean them up. The KGB, do you suppose?"

Svoboda's silence was the answer the German had expected.

"No, I didn't think so," Thadden answered his own question.

"You don't trust the Nazis?" He had almost said the Germans, but he caught himself in time.

"I trust myself," the ex-policeman from Berlin replied. "No personal offense."

"None taken."

"I believe I'll use the stairs."

"Till Friday night, then."

"*Ja.* And in the meantime, each man for himself."

IT WAS, Colonel Alexandrei Rostov thought, a relief to be alone once more. His comrades in the present venture made him nervous with their doubts and questions, a sensation he despised because it hinted at a hidden weakness in himself. It would have been much better, he thought, to use his own resources for the job, a KGB conspiracy from start to finish, but he needed cover if the plot went wrong.

The neo-Nazi Einsatzgruppe was his first line of defense, but his experience with Kolov had shown him it might not be good enough. Suppose the CIA or MI-6 *were* privy to the plan, at least in part. When it went through on schedule—or if something happened to prevent the strike—Rostov would need a human sacrifice to take the heat off himself. What better than a pair of disaffected swine from Prague and East Berlin, each hungry for revenge and anxious to recoup his past losses? The KGB couldn't be held responsible for every madman living in a former satellite.

He had no fear of Thadden or Svoboda telling what they knew to Western ears. It wouldn't come to that, the colonel knew. If necessary, he would silence both men on his own.

And if they were successful?

Rostov didn't share Svoboda's dream of a return to power by the Communists in Prague. He understood that it would take a Soviet invasion, like the crushing sweep of 1968, to reinstate a puppet government. The world might not sit still for that a second time, and with the German state united in an anti-Communist regime, the price of conquest might well be global war.

No need for that, in any case. His goal wasn't to reinstate the status quo of 1945, or even 1989. He would be content to spread disorder, rising doubts about the wisdom of détente and undermining any further moves toward *perestroika,* the absurd attempt to scuttle Communist ideals in favor of a Western mind-set. Certain fools in Moscow hadn't learned from history, the downfall of the British, French and American empires. It wasn't enough to put faith in revolutionary socialism while the world disintegrated right before your eyes. Swift action was required to salvage something from the mess before it was too late.

Already the USSR had been embarrassed—no, humiliated—in Afghanistan. Four decades of control in Eastern Europe had been shattered with the loss of Czechoslovakia, Hungary, Poland and East Germany. Now the Baltic states were gone and the economy was in severe distress. If the liberals had their way, the Soviet Union would go the way of the Ottoman Empire—the dustheap of history.

Rostov didn't suppose he could cure all those ills in one fell swoop, but he could make a start. The shock waves from the operation he had planned would be felt in Europe for generations to come, and while Rostov could never take public credit for the deed, his immediate superiors—some of them at least—would know the truth. He would be duly rewarded in time with advancement, especially if things went well and the degeneration of his country was checked.

But Colonel Rostov wasn't acting in the hope of a promotion or a pay raise. Rather, he was driven by a firm conviction that the people's revolution needed help. *His* help.

4

Emerging from the heated swimming pool, Gustave Lenart reflected on the strange turn his life had taken recently. For decades strict obedience had been his credo, the realities of politics a mild annoyance while he bent his mind to pure research. In astrophysics the established laws were cut and dried, immune to human temperament and avarice. The stars might not control man's destiny, but neither were they swayed by man's desire.

Lenart retrieved his towel and sat on a chaise longue, stretching out his legs. It would be cold outside, but the Rica Victoria hotel offered indoor swimming, along with a well-equipped game room and sauna facilities. It was a new experience, this traveling first class.

And soon he would be leaving it behind.

America was different, though. In Lenart's mind the whole country was first-class, with opportunities available to very man and woman. There were problems—anyone knew that—but he had trained himself to look beyond the daily propaganda he was used to. When Czechoslovakia had broken free of the Soviet yoke, he had been doing research in the USSR. Now, despite profound changes in the Soviet Union, a man with his secrets was still a valuable commodity, one the Russians weren't eager to let go.

Lenart had made his decision. The CIA wanted his special talents, and he wanted the safety of America. Czechoslovakia was still too close to the Russian bear for comfort.

"How's the water, Gustave?"

Vasily Kirov stood beside him, wearing a terry-cloth robe over his swimming trunks, carrying a thick towel folded across his arm.

"It's perfect," Lenart replied.

He could have done without the interruption, but he knew his colleague still felt out of place despite the hospitality they had been shown thus far in Norway. Kirov was a bookish man and knew little of the world beyond his lab and tiny flat in Moscow. Compared to Vasily, Lenart could almost see himself as a sophisticate.

"You haven't gone to dinner yet?"

"Not yet," Lenart replied.

"Perhaps we can go together then. In a little while?"

"Of course."

He had worked with Kirov for three years now, and he still knew little more about the man then he'd known when they were introduced. A widower, no children, he devoted every waking moment to his work . . . or so it seemed.

Could there be more to Vasily than met the eye?

Lenart suspected he was growing paranoid, a consequence of living in a system where deception and betrayal were encouraged, touted as the virtues of a patriot. All that had changed, of course, at least according to official statements, but Lenart had seen too much in forty-seven years to trust a government for anything. Reforms were easily announced and just as easily withdrawn when they served their purpose, lulling men and women into new complacency with promises of change.

A teenager when the Russian tanks had rolled into Prague and crushed the grand experiment of freedom, he could still remember bodies in the street, a student who had set himself on fire in front of television cameras as a plea and protest to the world.

All wasted.

So Lenart was leaving Europe now, and if it happened that his pessimism was misplaced, the changes real this time, he might return someday. But for the moment he would seek his future in America. If he survived the next three days.

He watched Kirov launch himself into a shallow dive, slicing through the water with hardly a splash. His colleague swam with long, sure strokes, surprising in a man whose major form of exercise was keying data into his computer. Just who was Vasily Kirov?

And what about himself? How many of his friends and colleagues would suspect he was planning to defect to the United States? With any luck at all the answer would be none. Lenart had done the best he could to hide his tracks, but there were always risks involved. A single careless word could cause him difficulty, even get him killed.

Enough. Precautions had been taken, and his contact would be trained in the security procedures necessary for a case like this. The main risk to Lenart right now was that anxiety might cause him to betray himself.

Rest easy. Take it one step at a time. Have faith.

His new life was around the corner, waiting for him, but Lenart would have to wait a while before he realized his dream. Some obstacles remained, but he wasn't about to change his mind and back out now. He had glimpsed the prize, and he would strive to capture it with every ounce of strength at his command.

It pleased him that his contact was a Czech expatriate. Her flight to freedom had occurred before the new reforms, which made her even more courageous, and she seemed to understand his motives for distancing himself from his homeland. At their single meeting, back in Moscow, she had been supportive, never condescending, offering straight answers to the questions that were preying on his mind.

He hadn't seen her yet in Norway, but he told himself it was just his second day in Lillehammer. He couldn't expect the CIA to baby-sit him every moment. It would be unnatural, inviting the suspicion of his colleagues and authorities.

Suppose he should announce his plan to start a new life in the West? What then? He was a highly valued scientist—false modesty wouldn't deny him that admission—and the Soviets would almost certainly resist his leaving, one way or another. If he forced the issue publicly, they might back down by all appearances, but he would still remain a target for retaliation when the newsmen went in search of other stories.

No. The way to do it was as planned. A clean break, out and gone before his plan was recognized. No one could reach him in America with agents of the CIA and FBI on guard.

And if they did somehow, it would still be worth it. Just to die in freedom, having tasted liberty before the end.

The morbid thought depressed him, and he concentrated on the brighter picture. Lying on the beach in sunshine. Florida or California—he couldn't decide. Perhaps Hawaii. Suntan oil and palm trees . . .

"You're right, Gustave. The water's perfect."

Kirov stood above him, toweling off. "You've finished swimming then?" he asked.

"Four laps. It's enough for now, I think."

"What time is it?"

The watch on Kirov's wrist was apparently waterproof. He wiped the face and answered, "Seven forty-three."

"It's late enough," Lenart replied. "I'm hungry now."

"The pepper steak was excellent last night."

"I'll see you in the dining room?"

"In just a little while."

Lenart would have preferred to dine alone, but sociability would cost him nothing on the eve of his departure for the West. He thought of Kirov as a little stuffy sometimes—make that *all* the time—but who among his scientific colleagues qualified as what the Americans would call a "party animal"? His chosen life-style was sedate by definition, almost cloistered, but Lenart decided that would change when he was safely on the other side.

The thought provoked a smile. He had begun to think of "crossing over" as an almost mystic art, like moving toward the afterlife. Except that he didn't believe in heaven or a world beyond the here and now.

This life was all he had, and he would make the best of what remained.

But first he had to reach America, and that meant getting out of Europe with his life. Lenart stood waiting for the elevator, wishing he believed enough to pray.

FORTY MILES DUE NORTH of Lillehammer, in the town of Tretten, the self-appointed warriors of the master race met at the Skeikampen hotel. Six men sat around a table, two of them in business suits, the other four in casual attire. They would have passed as businessmen and tourists at a glance, unless you focused on their eyes. No two resembled another physically, but all six had fanatics' eyes, the kind most often seen in mug shots taken by police.

"Reports," Eric Norner, the leader of the Einsatzgruppe said. At twenty-seven he appeared to be the perfect Aryan: blue eyes, blond hair, a chiseled profile. He could have been an advertisement for genetic engineering. Turning to the first man on his left, he said, "Begin please, Klaus."

"The weapons have arrived," Klaus Wagner said. "We were forced to bribe a Jew in customs, but there was no problem otherwise."

"All items are accounted for?"

"Yes. Some of the Uzis have been used before, but all are functional and in good condition. Extra pistols with the ammunition and grenades."

"I wish we had the time and place to test them." Dieter Koch was frowning as he spoke. The Einsatzgruppe's second-in-command had jet black hair, a thick mustache and pallid skin. He was a chronic worrier.

"You think we've been swindled, Dieter?" Norner asked.

"Anything can happen with a weapon," the man replied. "Weak springs, a faulty firing pin."

"I have assurances."

"From Beck?" He spoke the name of Norner's contact with an accent verging on disdain.

"From Beck. You don't trust him?"

"Trust," Dieter said, "is a luxury we can't afford."

"He hasn't failed us yet. The guns in Frankfurt, the plastique in Düsseldorf."

"It only takes one failure, Eric."

"So why don't you pick three guns at random from the shipment, take them to the woods tonight and try them out?"

Koch frowned and shook his head. "If *you* trust Beck..."

"I do. He knows what to expect if he betrays us." Norner faced the next of his lieutenants. "Josef?"

Josef Ziegler's face was riven by a scar across one cheek. He liked to blame it on a beating by police, but Norner knew it was the product of a drunken auto crash.

"No changes in the schedule," Ziegler said. "The conference will convene on Friday afternoon as planned. That evening everyone will gather in the Rica Victoria's dining room for greetings from the king."

"The uniforms?"

"All ready. They have taken on four extra waiters for the banquet," Ziegler reported. "I slipped some money to the manager in charge of personnel. He thinks I'm from the union, getting kickbacks from the temporary help.''

''The rest?''

''We have four rooms at the hotel as planned. On Friday night our men will bring their 'business colleagues' back for dinner in the public dining room for cocktails in the lounge. If we can't achieve success with thirteen guns, then we deserve to fail.''

''Reinhardt?''

Facing Norner from across the table, Reinhardt Klassen was the largest of the men in height and girth. His voice, by contrast, sounded like a whisper from a well.

''Escape routes double-checked and ready,'' he replied. ''By half-past seven I'll have the vehicles in place. Two crash cars to delay police in the event of pursuit. A sniper team across the street from the hotel for backup.''

''Excellent. And Werner?''

At thirty-eight Werner Heydrich was the oldest of the group. He had a proud tradition to uphold. His grandfather had been condemned to hang at Nuremberg for so-called ''crimes against humanity.''

''I've arranged for transport from Vangsnes. A ferry south to Bergen and from there to Wilhelmshaven. The boat will leave at dawn,'' he said to Ziegler. ''Don't be late.''

''Ten hours for two hundred fifty miles?'' The smile on Ziegler's face put crinkles in his scar. ''No problem.''

''One other thing,'' Koch said. ''The Denmark business.''

And it was Norner's turn to smile. He'd been saving this. A treat to whet their appetites. The Einsatzgruppe's third man on the scene at Legoland had packed a camera to document the kill. Instead, his lens had framed the likeness of an enemy, preserved for all eternity on film.

"I have good news, my brothers. Contacts have identified the bitch who murdered Fritz and Hans. A Czech now working for the CIA."

"Americans?" There was a note of disbelief in Heydrich's voice... or was it fear?

"You're surprised? The target was a Russian pig. America is ruled by Jews and Communists. They play at being enemies and then cooperate behind the scenes."

"Good news, you said."

"The bitch is here," Norner said. "She was seen in Lillehammer yesterday."

"But why?" Klassen asked.

"The Americans have people at the conference. They'd certainly demand security."

"Coincidence?" The scowl on Ziegler's face told Norner he wasn't convinced. "I smell a trap."

"A trap can work both ways. Sometimes the trapper winds up being caught himself."

"You have a plan?"

"Of course. The bitch will come and be our guest tomorrow. She'll tell us everything she knows, and if there's a risk we've overlooked, she'll prepare us for the worst. When we're finished with her... well, perhaps a sacrifice for Fritz and Hans."

Appreciative laughter from the troops. They all felt better now, though he could see Klassen still had res-

ervations. Clashing with police in Norway was a minor risk compared to dealing with the CIA, but Eric
Norner had no lack of confidence. If necessary, he'd
do the job himself. A martyr to the master race, im-
mortalized in legend for the pure-blood generations yet
unborn.

Inspired, he rose and stood before them, studying
the upturned faces. "Gentlemen," he said, "we have
an opportunity to strike a major blow against the Jews
and mongrels in our midst. We must not fail. Reunion
of the Fatherland has given us a sign. The time is ripe
to realize the dream of one who went before."

He didn't have to speak the Name. It was embla-
zoned in their minds. The warrior god of their de-
feated ancestors. A man they all revered.

"It's our fate to live in decadent, disordered times,
but we can change all that. Our strength and inspira-
tion shall not fail. I've heard it said that we were born
too late. The Reich was swept away before we had a
chance to stand and fight. But it is *not* too late!"

He had their full attention now, all eyes locked on his
face. "Our goal of racial purity can yet be realized if
we're strong enough to do our part. Already there's
trouble for the Russian pigs at home. Their puppet
states are crumbling around them like a house of cards.
The wheel of history is turning, brothers. It will grind
our enemies to dust."

There was a muted ring in his ears, and he could feel
the pounding rhythm of his pulse. Exhilaration
thrummed in his veins. "Our long, proud history will
not be pushed aside. Our destiny *will* be fulfilled." He
felt electric tension crackling in the air. "One race!"

They answered him as with a single voice. "One race!"

"One nation!"

On their feet they roared, "One nation!"

"One leader!"

Stiff arms lifted in salute. "One leader!"

The power of their warrior god infused him with newfound strength. *"Sieg heil!"*

"Heil Hitler!"

Tomorrow, he thought, was the beginning of a bright new day. "The king is dead," he proclaimed, beaming. "Long live the king!"

5

The digital alarm woke Bolan from a dreamless sleep at 6:00. He showered quickly, dressed and locked the bag that contained his surplus weapons. There was nowhere the warrior could safely hide the bag, so he left it in plain sight, together with his other luggage. If the room was searched while he was out, his cover would be blown, but he would count on any prowlers to avoid involvement with police.

The breakfast room was different from the one where he had dined with Monica the night before. There were broad windows to admit the morning light, with flowers on the tables and numbers matched to rooms for guests in residence. The hostess led him to a table on the far side of the room, and Bolan gave his order to a smiling waitress.

His dinner with the woman from the CIA had been uneventful, their time passed in general conversation, avoiding the details of their assignment. They'd meet again in the afternoon when Monica expected fresh intelligence, but Bolan had the morning free. Without a private contact in the city or a lead on how to find the members of the Einsatzgruppe, he was blocked from making a preemptive strike.

The clock was running on a deadline, but he still had no idea of where or when the neo-Nazi gunmen planned to strike. The conference seemed a likely target with the king on hand, but he couldn't be sure without some hard intelligence to back up the feeling. And if his guess was wrong...

He didn't want to think about the consequences of a fascist terror coup, with Europe so unsettled from the recent, sweeping tide of change. A scientist's defection paled next to the havoc such a raid might generate. Already there were rumblings of a far-right ground swell in the new, united Germany—from anti-Semitic vandalism and underground video games extolling the Holocaust to more overt political moves. The last thing anybody needed at the moment was a neo-Nazi fighting cadre on the loose, focusing old hatreds and providing extremists with a rallying point.

It had been his father's war, a different age, but Bolan recognized the scars that Hitler's juggernaut had left behind in Europe. Some of them might never heal entirely, but he was committed to prevention of a reoccurrence.

Savages were savages, regardless of the banners they adopted or the slogans they espoused. The Vietcong and KGB could teach the old Gestapo hands a trick or two about applied technology, but their voracious evil smelled the same to Bolan.

Rank corruption, and the stench of violent death.

His breakfast came and went, a filling meal that Bolan rarely tasted, since his mind was on other things. He signed the bill and charged it to his room, emerging just in time to catch a glimpse of Monica across the lobby. Going out.

His curiosity was instantly aroused. Why not? He had the morning free, and trailing her would be a way to occupy his time. Besides, if she had working contacts on the scene, he might be able to obtain some early pointers of his own.

It wasn't lack of trust precisely, but he knew that Monica—the CIA in general—had a separate agenda from his own. No matter how Brognola spelled it out, his job in Norway was more than just watching from the sidelines while a Czech defector made the move from East to West. His job meant seizing the initiative and using every means at his disposal to destroy the Einsatzgruppe before it spilled another drop of blood.

Perhaps today.

He gave Monica a fair head start, slipping out of the hotel in time to see her walking north along the street. No taxi, then. He fell in step behind her, hanging back the best part of a block to give her room. If she was watching out for tails, he didn't want to give himself away.

And, on the other hand, if she was being tailed by someone else, he stood at least a fifty-fifty chance of smoking out the enemy.

More paranoia? Bolan didn't think so. They had three men dead already, and the body count was bound to rise within the next few hours. It was inescapable, with neo-Nazis in the woodwork and the KGB on standby, waiting in the wings. But for the moment he had morning sunshine, peace and quiet on a scenic avenue with Monica in sight.

Don't knock it, Bolan thought. The heat would come down soon enough. And when it did, he'd need all his skill to keep from getting burned.

Monica knew Lenart's room number at the Rica Victoria, and she also knew enough to avoid the room itself in case of spies. Instead, she called first, using the number without Lenart's name, asking for somebody else when he answered. Playing innocent—a simple wrong number—and slipping in the code word when she had a chance before ringing off.

It was a simple tactic, mapped out in advance. Upon receipt of such a call Lenart would leave the hotel and make directly for a nearby park, observing whether he was followed to the meet. Monica, meanwhile, would scan the area for obvious—or not so obvious—surveillance, prior to making contact with Lenart.

It worked on paper, but she knew that real life had a way of complicating plans. At Legoland, for instance, where a simple hand-off had become a massacre and she'd nearly lost her life.

But not this time. She was carrying the Walther, smuggled into Norway in the bottom of a check-through suitcase, and an extra magazine weighed down the pocket of her stylish jacket. Legoland had been the first time she had ever killed a man, and while she kept waiting for shock or depression to set in, they never came.

She didn't *like* the feeling, relish the experience, but neither was she traumatized. It had been self-defense, and Monica had seen enough of unjustified brutality and killing to make the difference plain.

Still, the last thing she needed right now was more violence, here in the heart of peaceful Lillehammer. It wouldn't blow their transfer necessarily, but any heat at all would be unwelcome.

The park was green and spacious, relatively free of foot traffic at this hour of the morning. On a Thursday most Norwegians would be off to work or on their way to school, and shops wouldn't be opening to serve the tourists for another thirty minutes yet. It was the quiet time, except for traffic flowing past, and even that was somewhat muted as she made her way into the park.

The last time she'd seen this man in Moscow he'd been nervous—even frightened—but determined to proceed. As a top-rated astrophysicist, he was a man the Soviets, reforms or not, would be reluctant to let go. A man who might not even be safe in his native Czechoslovakia. Understandably the man felt he'd be safer in the States.

Lenart was waiting for her on a bench, with trees behind him serving as a kind of screen. Of half a dozen others she could see, none seemed to give the astrophysicist a second glance, and none was packing cameras or bags that could conceal recording gear.

So far so good.

It was a risk, regardless, but they had to speak, and she couldn't afford to talk about their business on the telephone. It was absurdly simple to penetrate a hotel switchboard, and even leaving the hotel wouldn't solve the problem if Lenart was trailed by spotters armed with directional microphones. This way at least she had a chance to judge his state of mind and temperament, examine his resolve and satisfy herself that he was ready for the move.

She approached Lenart obliquely, trying to make it look casual, aware that trained watchers would immediately see through her charade. She sat on the opposite end of his bench, with space for two more bodies in between them, checking out the bushes one last time before she spoke.

"You're looking well," she said to him in English.

"Better than I feel perhaps."

"What's wrong?"

"A touch of stage fright, I suppose. It's really happening."

"That's right. It is."

"A part of me is sad, reluctant. Do you understand?"

"I felt the same when it was my time." And she had, but that was over now. "At least you have no family to leave behind."

"A blessing, yes?" There was a bitter irony behind his words.

"I only mean—"

"You're right, of course. Forgive my mood."

"There's nothing to forgive," she told him, meaning it.

"How soon?"

"On Saturday. Your seminars break up at five o'clock, I understand."

"According to the published schedule, yes. Unfortunately scientists are always windy. It could take another twenty, thirty minutes to escape the clutches of a lecturer."

"No problem. We'll be ready for the move at four o'clock and any time thereafter. I'll be spotting in the lobby when you're done."

She knew the critical importance of a familiar face. It would have thrown Lenart off-stride to bring a stranger in too close when he was worried by the prospect of surveillance from the other side.

"What then?"

"You'll have some papers from the seminar? Some notes or handouts?"

"Certainly. They generate a paper blizzard at conventions."

"If you're ready, tuck them under your right arm, folded. I'll take care of passing on the word."

"And if I'm not prepared?"

She frowned. "You won't be bringing any luggage, Doctor. I'll assume a no-go means you've spotted a surveillance team, or you have some other problem that requires a remedy."

"Of course. I understand."

"If we're rolling, wait ten minutes from the time you see me in the lobby, then come back to this location. Nothing complicated, just a walk to stretch your legs before you dress for dinner."

"Yes, all right."

"A car will make one pass precisely on the ten-minute mark, and again five minutes later if you aren't in place. They can't keep circling the park, however. You must understand that time is the essence."

"Certainly. One thing..."

"Go on."

"One of my colleagues has, how do you say, attached himself to me. I think he's lonely. If he attempts to join me on my little walk—"

"Prevent him, Doctor. Say you have a headache, anything at all. Be rude if necessary. We don't have accommodations for another passenger, and anyone we leave behind can pass along descriptions of the car, the pickup team, you name it.''

''So.''

''We also have a fallback option.''

''Yes?''

''I won't go into detail now, but it involves an ambulance. In case you're physically prevented from proceeding with our plan tomorrow afternoon, don't think I'll abandon you.''

''I never thought . . .''

He let it trail away, and the expression on his face told Monica the truth. He *had* considered being left behind, discarded if the plan went wrong. It was a natural concern, and she could tell that he had pictured various scenarios. Exposure. Ridicule at best. At worst . . . ? Would the ''new'' Russia charge him with leaking secrets to the West?

''Just stick to the procedure,'' Monica advised him. ''I won't let you down.''

''Tomorrow, then?''

''Tomorrow.''

He left first, and Monica remained in place for several moments, watching pigeons forage in the shrubbery. No hurry now.

Five minutes passed before she rose and started back to her hotel.

''THE BITCH IS COMING NOW.''

''She doesn't look like much,'' Josef Ziegler said, staring through the windshield of the hired sedan.

''What does it take to pull a trigger?'' one of his commandos questioned from the rear.

''A little nerve for one thing. She looks . . . weak.''

"She murdered Fritz and Hans," the driver said.

"I'm not forgetting that. It's why we're here."

"Let's do it then."

"A moment. Bide your time."

He had no doubt the four of them could do the job. A simple pickup on the street, and they were gone. If there was any trouble from the woman, he had a blackjack and a plastic bag filled with cotton wadding and soaked in chloroform. Sweet dreams or headaches, either way.

They would have taken her before she had reached the park, but she was on the wrong side of the street and there was too much traffic, people on their way to work, and any kind of a major snarl would bring policemen running. In the park itself there was an old man on the bench beside her. They didn't appear to speak, but Ziegler had refused to make a second pass or grab the woman in circumstances where his men would have to run a minimum of fifty yards and back again.

Too risky. Too much wasted time.

Returning to the Oppland, if he didn't miss his guess, the woman would be on their side of the street, and they could run up on her blind side for an easy grab. She might be armed, of course, but that couldn't be helped. They had surprise and numbers going for them, plus the zeal of trained, committed warriors in a holy cause. They wouldn't fail.

It would be easier to gun her down, pay back the deaths of Fritz and Hans in kind and get it over with. But Norner wanted this one for interrogation, and the wisdom of his choice hadn't been lost on Ziegler. Women like the blonde didn't consort with Russian agents on their own. She had to have superiors, and even if they had been ignorant about the Einsatz-gruppe prior to Legoland, her people would be curious by now. Two bodies on their hands, well known from wanted posters in the Fatherland and elsewhere.

There were questions to be answered, and he trusted Eric Norner, with his bosom buddy Koch, to find the answers.

"Get ready."

"We've *been* ready," one of the commandos muttered from behind him.

In another situation Ziegler would have called the soldier on it, maybe even slapped his face, but this wasn't the time. His mind was focused on the sole objective of the woman, rolling up behind her as she moved along the sidewalk, passed a bookstore, a druggist's, an appliance shop. She seemed to *feel* them coming, and he knew it was time.

"Go *now!*"

The driver braked and doors sprang open, boot heels clomping on the pavement. Ziegler saw the woman turning, reaching underneath her jacket as she made the move. That quickly he knew why Fritz and Hans were dead.

He poked his head and one arm through the window, shouting, "Watch her hands!"

They might be forced to kill her now, and Norner wouldn't be amused.

THE TRICK HAD BEEN not trailing Monica inside the park. Instead, he circled wide around to intercept her if she came out on the other side, already guessing that a meet was going down. He didn't have a prayer of learning who or why unless he moved in close enough that he could see her. Meaning *she* could see *him,* too.

No dice.

It troubled Bolan, but he understood where Monica was coming from. The CIA had rules, procedures, that its agents were required to follow. He could think of several explanations for the meet, all logically related to Lenart's defection. There was no reason to suspect duplicity, certainly no reason why she should have briefed him on the contact in advance.

Still, if it had some bearing on the Einsatzgruppe, he would have liked to glimpse her contact, maybe trail the new face when they finished, letting Monica go back to the hotel alone. If he could spot her leaving, make a hasty sweep for anyone who split about the same time, it could still work out.

Perhaps.

He killed time window-shopping, keeping one eye on the park, and he was ready when Lenart emerged. The physicist looked older than he did in Hal Brognola's photographs, more drawn and haggard. Bolan knew he was in his forties, but he could have passed for ten years older, anyway.

Stress kills, he thought. Provided you lived that long.

There was no point in following Lenart. He'd be heading back to his hotel, and Bolan had no interest in the man beyond the task of overseeing his transfer to the West. He waited, moving down the street a bit to make himself less obvious when Monica returned.

It was a gamble, knowing she might just as easily slip out the other way and keep another rendezvous—or several—while he killed time covering the park, but Bolan stood a greater chance of missing her by giving up his post. When she appeared some moments later, he was waiting in a shadowed doorway, giving her a block before he fell into step behind.

If he was grading her on countermeasures, Bolan would have given Monica a failing grade. She hadn't checked her backtrack once that he could tell. No trips around the block or sudden pauses, checking window merchandise and meanwhile glancing back to see if anyone seemed just a bit *too* casual about ignoring her. In truth he couldn't tell if she was negligent or so damn good she could check her tail without appearing to. In that case, though, it was virtually certain she'd be aware of Bolan trailing her.

What then?

He could explain it was a friendly exercise, or he could tell the truth. They had their separate agendas, but cooperation didn't mean Bolan was required to sit around the Oppland, sitting on his hands while Monica went out to work the streets.

No way.

In fact, it might be best if he—

The gray sedan fell into place behind, slowing enough that Monica remained a pace or two ahead. He recognized the car, or thought he did, from the reverse trip. It had flickered past him, one of many rolling in the other lane, and kept on going when he reached the park.

Four men inside the car.

He watched the back doors open, two hulks rushing toward the sidewalk, Monica just noticing and turning back to face them as they charged. If she was quick and had a black belt in kung fu, she might delay them long enough for Bolan to assist. If not . . .

But she didn't adopt a fighting stance, per se. Instead, she reached inside her jacket in a move he recognized. And so did someone in the car.

A voice cried "Watch her hands!" It was the proper thing to do, all things considered, but the runners hesitated for a heartbeat, taking in the woman's movement and the shouted order from the car. Before they knew it Monica had drawn an automatic pistol, aiming at the bruiser on her right.

He gave them credit for a swift, professional response. The hulking target raised his hands at once, while number two dodged farther to her left, then cut back in a zigzag pattern, crouching low. As Monica swung back to cover him, the first man made his move.

She shot the zigzag runner at a range of twelve or fifteen feet, the popping sound of gunfire sharp and loud in Bolan's ears. He palmed the new Beretta, thumbing back the hammer as he ran, prepared for anything.

The first shot rocked her target, but it didn't stop his charge. He staggered into Monica and spoiled her second shot, a window shattering behind him as the bullet missed its mark. By that time his companion had already closed the gap and seized her gun arm, twisting painfully until her automatic clattered onto the sidewalk.

"Hey!"

It was the best Bolan's mind could offer in the circumstances, concentrating on his footwork and the two men remaining in the car. He caught a glance from one of Monica's assailants, while the other tried to cope with both a clawing, kicking woman and a bleeding shoulder wound.

Good luck.

The front door on the gray sedan swung open, and a husky shooter with an Uzi in his hands unfolded from the shotgun seat. There was perhaps a second to decide, and the Executioner registered a facial scar before he shot the man three times, a rising pattern to the chest and throat. The impact pitched Bolan's target backward, and he lost the Uzi somewhere on his way toward contact with the gutter.

Monica's attackers saw the writing on the wall, but there was no escape hatch. One—the man with the shoulder wound—was digging underneath his leather jacket for a weapon when the Executioner squeezed off a parabellum round and punched his nose back toward his brain stem.

One to go, and then the wheelman lost it, standing on the gas and accelerating out of there, with three doors flapping like a set of broken wings.

The lone attacker made a running dive at the sedan and almost missed. Almost. He kissed the bumper going down and wound up rolling on the pavement, struggling to his hands and knees.

No time to waste. A parabellum round drilled through the would-be kidnapper's forehead and flipped him over onto his back. By the time Bolan reached Monica Jakes, she had retrieved her pistol and was staring at him with a strange expression.

"How—"

"No time," he snapped. "Unless you want to chat with the police, we have to move. Right now."

6

They returned to the Oppland hotel by a circuitous route, dodging down an alley fifty feet from the shooting scene, slowing to a walk when they reached the first parallel street. By that time Monica had found her voice.

"You followed me!" There was more than a hint of anger in her tone.

"You're welcome."

"Why?"

"Something to do. From the way it worked out it's a good thing I did."

She flicked a glance at Bolan, eyes like emerald fire. "I could have handled it!"

"It's handled."

"One of them escaped."

"I didn't have a shot. Win some, lose some."

She thought about another tart reply but caught herself in time. "I'm sorry, honestly. You saved my life."

"My pleasure."

Sirens whooped in the distance, racing toward the kill site. Bolan watched for police cars, but they were still in the clear. He couldn't rule out witnesses, a shopkeeper perhaps, but with the violence and confusion he had no great fear of accurate descriptions. Still, he'd feel better when they reached the Oppland and were off the street.

"They didn't want Lenart," Monica said.

"Unless all four of them were blind, I'd say you're right."

"But why? I mean, who even knows I'm here?"

"You mean, aside from Langley and Lenart, the hotel staff..."

"And you. Your people."

"Put your mind at ease on that score. All I knew before we met was that I had a contact waiting. Female, sure, but there was nothing in way of names or details."

"Who then?"

"Off the top I see two options. Someone interested in Lenart, or someone with a personal grudge against you."

"What sort of grudge?"

"Dead Nazis maybe."

"Impossible. How would they find me here?"

"Same way they found your contact when they made the hit in Denmark. Someone set it up."

"That's different. I was dealing with a Russian. Anyone at his end could have stumbled onto information and arranged the contract."

Bolan shrugged. "I'd say you've got two choices. It's either the Einsatzgruppe or the Reds. Somebody made you, and they want you taken off the board. It's crude, but still effective."

"I was careful," Monica replied. "I don't believe it possible that I was followed here from Denmark."

"Then they knew you were coming," Bolan told her, playing on the obvious.

She got the point at once, and he saw angry color rising in her cheeks. "You have no right to say that!"

"I'm not pointing any fingers, Monica. You have to ask yourself who profits if the Einsatzgruppe pulls its stunt on schedule."

"The hard-liners in Moscow."

"Right. And anybody else with an investment in the cold war. Who got hit the hardest when the walls came down?"

"You think the Company—"

"I didn't say that. Langley called my people in, remember."

"And I still don't know exactly who 'your people' are."

"With any luck you never will."

"You talk in riddles."

"If I had a name to offer you, I'd make a call and have him taken out. It's not that simple."

"But if Langley didn't..." Monica's frustration was apparent as she left the sentence hanging, incomplete. "For God's sake, *who?*"

"It wouldn't be the first time there were rogues who acted on their own," Bolan said. "Just a possibility, but something you should keep in mind. Somebody with a stake in turning up the heat and everything to lose if peace breaks out."

They reached the Oppland moments later, passing on the elevator at Bolan's suggestion. The first stop was Monica's room, a floor below Bolan's, and they both had pistols ready as she turned the key. He half expected to discover chaos in the room, with evidence of hasty searching, but the place was spotless.

"Damn!" she said. "You've made me paranoid."

"I'm not the one who tried to snatch you off the street."

"You're right. I'm sorry."

"Skip it," Bolan said. "If I were you..."

"Go on." For once she didn't seem to take offense. "What would you do if you were me?"

"I'd concentrate on strategy right now. Nothing major, just revise your plans enough to throw the spotters off if they've been briefed on what they should expect."

"The transfer..."

Bolan shook his head. "There's nothing you can do about that now without alerting Langley. If you scrub the drivers and the rest of it, they'll want to plan another drop. You're right back where you started."

"So?"

"You need a test," he told her. "Something you can feed to your control without upsetting any major plans. Sit back and see what happens. If the heavies show, you'll know you've got a problem."

"Wonderful. The conference starts tomorrow afternoon."

"I never said it would be easy."

Monica was slipping off her jacket when she grimaced at a sudden stab of pain.

"Are you all right?"

"Some stiffness. And a bruise, I think. If you hadn't been watching..."

"Maybe you could use a breather," he suggested.

"I could use a sauna," she replied. And then she asked offhandedly, "Why don't you join me? I mean, you can help me plan the sort of test I should use with my control."

"I'll need to change, stop by my room."

"Go now. I'll meet you there in ten minutes."

"Fine."

He used the same precautions at his own door, braced for anything, but once again the maid had been the only visitor. His suitcase arsenal was still intact, a hair protruding from the keyhole of the left-hand latch where he'd left it, certain to dislodge if anybody tried to pick the lock.

Okay.

He stripped down to his shorts and slipped on a terry robe and sandals, picking out a bath towel that would cover the Baretta on his way downstairs. The sauna was a basement fixture, and he rode the elevator down, already hoping they'd have it to themselves. He found Monica there ahead of him, hanging her robe on a wall hook. A towel was wrapped around her, covering her body from the armpits to the upper thighs.

"It seems we're all alone," she told him. "I believe it's safe to talk."

"Should be."

The layout boasted two whirlpools, half a dozen shower stalls, two saunas on the left and two more on the right. They took the nearest one, and Bolan closed the wooden door behind them. It was as hot as hell inside, a dry heat that was instantly replaced with rising steam when Monica poured water on a brazier filled with heated stones. They sat together, touching-close, on risers that reminded Bolan of the bleachers at a ballpark.

Bolan felt ridiculous in shorts, already sweated through, and Monica couldn't resist a smile at his discomfort.

"Why not take those off and wear the towel . . . or not, if you prefer. It's considered proper, even by the strictest of Norwegians."

Bolan smiled. "I brought the towel for this as much as anything." He opened it and let her see the gun.

"We should be safe enough."

"I wouldn't be so sure."

She smiled. "I think you're bashful."

"That's a new one. I've been called a lot of things, but bashful never made the list."

She stood and dropped her towel, ignoring Bolan as she bent, stark naked, to arrange it on the bench. He tore his eyes away as Monica resumed her seat.

"That's better. With a sauna it's best to open up the pores."

"Okay."

"Now you."

"My pores are doing fine."

"You have me at a disadvantage now," she told him, teasing, "and it really isn't fair."

Resigned, he skinned off the shorts and sat down, knees pressed together. Bolan wondered how much of the heat he felt was coming from the sauna, and how much he was generating on his own.

"That's right," Monica said. "Now if another guest should happen by, he won't be suspicious."

"In the States they'd raid this place."

"But we aren't doing anything."

Was it imagination, or was Monica a little closer now?

"About the plan." She turned to face him, making no attempt to hide herself.

"It doesn't have to be elaborate," he replied, and wondered where the hell the croaking voice had come from. "I assume you check in periodically?"

"Of course."

"So next time drop a word about the snatch...I mean, the problem. Just to get the point across that it didn't work. You've got a local contact working on some answers, but you don't need any help. A meeting's been arranged. You pick the time and place, no cover, but you're telling them in case it sours. We stake out the site from someplace safe, and if the bad guys make a personal appearance, then you know you've got a leak."

"You've obviously done this kind of thing before."

"It beats a knife between the shoulder blades," Bolan said. "If I'm wrong, we waste a little time and you report back that your contact hasn't gotten the information yet."

"And if you're right...about the leak, I mean?"

"Depends on who shows up, how many, what they're packing. It could go all kinds of ways."

"I see."

"You mind a personal question?"

"If I mind, I need not answer."

"Fair enough. What made you choose the Company, with all you'd been through beforehand?"

"That's exactly *why* I made the choice. A life of trusting no one in my native land, it seemed I should try to make a difference if I could. Sometimes our dreams don't come true."

"Sometimes they change," Bolan said, "as we go along."

"Perhaps. It's ironic that I now mistrust my own superiors."

"I could be wrong," the Executioner replied.

"But you don't think so."

"I'll be satisfied to wait and see."

"A question of my own."

"Okay."

"What made *you* choose this life?"

"In the beginning," Bolan said, "I had a job to do. My duty. I was younger. It was wartime."

"Vietnam?"

"To start. Wars change, the names and faces, but it didn't take that long to realize the enemy was still the same. We get hung up on flags sometimes and lose track of the men behind them."

"I believe we understand each other."

Bolan hoped so, but he didn't want to press his luck.

"I haven't thanked you properly," she said.

"For what?"

"My life."

"Let's say I had a selfish motive."

"Yes?"

"I'd hate to do the whole thing by myself."

"A hard man, yes?"

"I'm getting there."

She smiled and ran her fingernails along his thigh. "If there's anything I can do to help..."

"I wouldn't be surprised."

THE TELEPHONE DISTRACTED Vasily Kirov, drawing his attention from the scientific journal in his hands. He frowned, considering the instrument as if it were a hostile entity. He could ignore it, make the caller think he was out, but that wouldn't be wise. No one would call him here unless . . .

"Hello?"

"You recognize my voice?"

"Of course."

"This is an open line."

That much was obvious, and Kirov saw no need for a response. He waited for the too-familiar voice to make its point.

"Are you prepared?"

And there it was.

"I am."

"We might require assistance, after all."

A sudden tingling raised the short hairs on his nape. "I understand."

"There is a woman . . ."

Kirov listened to the rest of it, required to read between the lines at times because his caller wouldn't risk specifics on an open line when anyone might overhear. For all intents and purposes their conversation was innocuous, a simple plea for one friend to assist another with a problem that was never specified. The woman was described in general terms, but Kirov still felt confident that he would recognize her if and when the need arose.

When he replaced the handset in its cradle, he was tingling with excitement. It wasn't an order yet, but he was placed on notice that his services might be required upon a moment's notice. Not the scientific knowledge he was noted for—his *other* skill.

The one for which he'd shown an early aptitude in childhood. It had been recognized by agents of the state and channeled into more constructive avenues before he'd let his passion ruin everything. The state had given him a chance to lead two lives at once, both equally fulfilling in their separate ways, and it was ludicrous to think that any proclamation from a band of upstart peasants could destroy his world.

The men who had sheltered Kirov, training him and giving him the periodic opportunities to vent his lust and rage without reprisal, still existed. They couldn't be swept aside so easily.

He was a genius *and* a killer, one of... what? Perhaps a dozen in the world. A special breed with talents that could just as easily have landed him in prison at a research post in Moscow. It had taken the KGB to recognize his value on a level unrelated to his textbooks and computers. When the time came, after he was trained and ready, he'd shown them all what he could do.

In East Berlin.

In Poland.

Once in France.

No one suspected bookish scientists of looking much beyond their laboratories. The Americans derided them as "eggheads" and dismissed them out of hand once they delivered their reports in a language most men couldn't hope to understand. It was the same in Moscow and everywhere else he had been. Respect, but once removed. An athlete or an actor had more value to the masses than a man who used his brain. How startled all of them would be to know the truth.

Some day perhaps. But not today.

He'd be ready when—not "if"—the next call came. And he'd do the job he was paid to do. With pleasure.

Gustave Lenart was a dangerous fool. He listened to the talk of "freedom" and "reform," believing any change was for the better. He'd never understand that "freedom" was a hollow word, filled with different meanings by the men who used it. Kirov's freedom had nearly been swept away by the recent changes in the Soviet Union, and he meant to preserve his position by any means. Even if it meant killing his "friend" Gustave Lenart.

7

Bolan kept the shower cold and let the icy jets of water drum against his upturned face until his skin felt raw. A measure of his strength was coming back, the wilted feeling sloughing off by gradual degrees. A few more minutes and he might not feel like death warmed over.

Monica had taken him by surprise in more ways than one. Making love in the sauna—and again in the Jacuzzi—had left him physically drained, a combination of steam heat and physical exertion.

He knew the risks of getting close for all concerned, but there were moments in the hellgrounds when you either took the chance or let the moment pass you by. The chance was taken now, and he couldn't undo it, though he wouldn't have changed it if he had the power. Still . . .

He pushed the thought aside and concentrated on the moment, toweling off and moving toward the bedroom. Monica was in her own room and waiting for him. She'd make the call when he arrived, and they'd see.

See what?

He felt an urge to call Brognola, air his new suspicion of a leak at Langley, but he let it go. He couldn't monitor Brognola's progress, any more than the big

Fed could tell him what to do in Norway from one moment to the next. The team at Stony Man Farm had ample problems as it was; the last thing they needed was a covert rumble with the CIA. He was on his own for now, as usual.

Check that. He had an ally in the lady spook, but he'd have to watch his step in that regard if it turned out she was compromised by her superiors. And they'd know that answer soon enough.

He slipped the unfamiliar shoulder rigging on over a clean shirt, adjusting it slightly for a better fit. Not bad. He missed the Beretta 93-R, with its 20-round mag and capacity for 3-round auto bursts, but transatlantic packing was a bitch these days, the more so with precautions formulated in the wake of Operation Desert Storm. Still, Langley always had a way of coming up with hardware when you least expected it.

The MP-5K submachine gun had its own sling, with a swivel mount, and Bolan was relieved to find it didn't cramp his style to wear both weapons simultaneously. In the mirror it appeared that he was putting on a pound or two, but he'd pass a casual inspection. Anyone who tried to pat him down tonight was in for a surprise, and no mistake.

He got a fresh hair from his brush and rigged the suitcase latch once more to warn him if a prowler tampered with the extra ammunition and grenades. As for the rest, he had his passport in the side pocket of his jacket with a fair amount of traveler's checks. The rest of Bolan's cash reserve was locked up in the hotel safe, where he could reach it anytime.

The warrior checked his watch. He was ahead of schedule, even though it felt as if time were creeping by.

Five minutes remained before he was supposed to meet with Monica downstairs, and Bolan planned on being punctual.

He thought about the bungled kidnapping attempt, wishing he had a way of checking out the dead. The media might not release affiliations if the heat was on, and Bolan needed information on his enemies to help prepare for a defense. Monica's Company contacts would certainly have access to the information from police...but could he trust their answers when the chips were down? The alternative meant ringing someone's chimes at Stony Man, the very same involvement he was trying to avoid if possible.

But *was* it possible?

Brognola had recruited Bolan, after all, and information from the war room in Virginia had been used to sell the mission. Stony Man was in, no matter how he tried to talk his way around it. But could he afford to wait a few more hours, looking for a resolution to the question of a leak on Monica's side of the board. And if the leak proved out, then he'd have to make a choice: involve Brognola's people, or attempt to do it on his own.

And how would Monica react if there turned out to be a leak? It was another case of wait-and-see, but Bolan had a feeling in his gut on that score. Monica Jakes was a team player, all right, but she'd chosen the team—and the country—with a specific agenda in mind. Unless he missed his guess, divided loyalties at the top would leave some room for second thoughts, perhaps a reevaluation of her choice.

Two minutes. Close enough.

He locked the door behind him, moving toward the elevator, then decided once again to use the stairs. He didn't mind the extra bit of exercise, and any hypothetical assailants on the floor below would have their eyes—and guns—trained on the elevator doors. The stairs gave Bolan room to move if he encountered any opposition on the way. Inside an elevator you were trapped, as good as dead.

A vain precaution as it happened. There was no one on the service stairs or in the hall when he arrived on Monica's floor. A rookie might have felt self-conscious, even foolish, but the Executioner had learned to take precautions when and where he could. You couldn't count on second chances in a game of life and death.

MONICA ANSWERED the knock on her door with the Walther in hand, prepared to fire on an unfamiliar face. It bothered her a bit, this willingness to kill, but she consoled herself with a reminder that her opposition made the rules. She was relieved when she saw Mike Belasko's face. "You're right on time."

"We aim to please."

His voice did something to her, raising echoes of their recent, fevered coupling. "You've done all right so far," she told him, standing on her toes to kiss him lightly on the lips.

"The call?"

All business. That was good. It kept her mind on track, reminding her who she was and why they were together in the first place.

"Yes." She dialed the number, waited, heard it answered on the second ring. A businesslike voice gave the corporate name that tipped her off which daily password she should use. "Consumer research calling. Mr. Ragland, please."

"One moment."

She'd never met her contact in the flesh, but Monica imagined him as small and gray—gray suits, gray hair, gray skin from loitering indoors all day. She pictured him small, perhaps a trifle undernourished, but she understood the power he represented. He could make one call and have her mission terminated—have *her* terminated if it came to that.

And she was moved to wonder whether "Mr. Ragland" had already made that call.

"Hello?" The same gray voice.

"Consumer research here. An open line, sir."

"Just a moment, please."

She pictured "Ragland" punching buttons, working on a sweep. With the equipment he possessed it would be possible to spot the most sophisticated tap.

"Seems all right," the gray voice told her. "Can I help you?"

"Possibly. I had an unexpected interview this morning, following the one we prearranged."

"Oh, yes?" The tension in his voice was audible, but still controlled. Was he surprised to hear from Monica at all, or simply by her news?

"It all worked out," she said. "Some debits on the ledger, I'm afraid, but we're intact." Despite her contact's clearance of the line, they kept to the charade.

"I understand. You'll be proceeding with the overall promotion then?"

"Yes, sir." The gamble now. "I feel obligated to double-check my information first, however."

"Sensible. I quite agree."

"I've got a meeting on tonight, in fact. The Holmenkollen restaurant at nine o'clock."

"Do you require a sales rep for your presentation?"

"No, sir. I'd prefer to do this on my own."

"Of course. You have our utmost confidence. Do keep in touch."

"Yes, sir."

The line went dead, but Monica held on for several seconds longer, listening for any telltale clicks or other sounds that might suggest a tap that "Ragland" missed somehow. Forget it. Even if he dropped the ball, technology was too sophisticated these days to expect a sound of heavy breathing on the line.

"All done," she told Bolan, feeling both uneasy and a little sad.

"So now we wait."

A little over seven hours. Six, if she considered the necessity of leaving early to select a lookout post.

"I'd rather not be here alone," she said, "if that's all right."

Bolan didn't speak, but went to her and took her into his arms.

"Can we get rid of these?" she asked him, hands recoiling from the contact with his weapons.

"I imagine so."

"In fact..." Her nervous fingers found his belt. "We could get rid of this, as well."

"Sounds fair."

Forgetting for a time. And in the present circumstances it was all she could hope for. Speeding time along while life stood still.

THERE WAS AN ALLEY opposite the Holmenkollen restaurant, complete with shadows, garbage Dumpsters and the smell of urban alleys everywhere. They were in place by half-past seven, fortified by coffee and a filling meal, prepared to spend the next few hours waiting for an enemy who might not show his face.

And if the plan fell through, then what?

In theory it would clear Monica's contact, while leaving vital questions unanswered. Letting Langley off the hook meant someone from the other side had tracked her, broken through her cover and decided it was time to take her out. Of the alternatives, if Bolan had a choice, he thought he preferred a simple, home-grown traitor to a seemingly omniscient enemy.

No matter how she tried Monica was unable to pinpoint a time or place where her cover had broken down. She could recall no fumbles of her own, and while that didn't absolutely rule out personal mistakes, it narrowed down the field.

It was time to watch and wait.

The rental car was Monica's, and she was buckled in behind the wheel, with Bolan in the shotgun seat. They had a clear view of the restaurant, with no great risk of being seen themselves unless their enemies checked out the alley first . . . or tried to use it for themselves.

At 9:02 a gray sedan with a familiar look about it stopped outside the restaurant. Three men unloaded, checked the street and went inside.

"You make the car?" Bolan asked.

"Yes. It's the same."

"Get ready then."

She cupped the vehicle's dome light with her hand as Bolan exited and swiftly closed the door. The doomsday numbers echoed in his head, reminding him that they had only moments to effect the grab.

The driver had his window down and was smoking, half-turned toward the restaurant. A careless move. He swiveled toward Bolan when the sound of running footsteps reached him, but the movement came too late. A chop with the Beretta, and he folded, lost his cigarette somewhere between his feet and toppled slowly to his right.

The Executioner was on a roll. He opened the driver's door and gave a shove, the deadweight resisting for a moment, then finally scooting over far enough to let him in. A curl of smoke now rose from the carpet, and he crushed the cigarette beneath his heel. He powered out of there, a smooth run through the gears, aware of Monica's headlights behind him as he reached across and took a Browning automatic from the snoozing driver's belt.

It pleased him, thinking of the other three when they emerged, frustrated, from the restaurant. No targets visible, and then no wheels.

He drove down to the lakefront, Monica behind him all the way. The ferries didn't run at night, and it was dark along the pier. A perfect place for work that wouldn't stand the light of day.

He parked and killed the engine, Monica's rental pulling in two car lengths back. She'd been anxious to participate in the interrogation, but he talked her out of it by noting that the move would leave her car unmanned, perhaps unreachable if they were interrupted by police . . . or worse. Reluctantly she sat behind the wheel and waited, watching huddled silhouettes inside the gray sedan.

He grabbed one of the driver's ears and twisted hard, repeating the maneuver twice before his captive came around with muttered curses, slapping at his hand.

"Do you speak English?"

"Ja."

"So speak it!"

"Yes. I understand you."

"Out. This side."

The driver followed him, still groggy, stepping to the side and leaning back against the car as Bolan closed the door.

"Your name?"

"Fuck you."

Bolan stuck the Browning in the wheelman's face. The German blinked when he saw the cold glint in the Executioner's eyes. "Wrong answer. Try again."

The man coughed and muttered an obscenity. Bolan lightly stroked the trigger of the gun, causing the German to gulp. "I'm waiting," he growled.

"You are the police?" the man croaked.

"I'll ask the questions. Your name?"

"Peter."

"Are you with the Einsatzgruppe?"

"I have rights."

All Bolan had to do was look at the man this time.

"Die Einsatzgruppe, ja."

"I need a quick word with your boss. Where would I find him, Peter?"

The driver read his death in Bolan's face and answered up, providing a street address in Lillehammer, and another one in Tretten to the north. There was no way to stash his subject while he checked him out, and they were running out of time in any case.

"Okay, take off," he told the rattled man.

The driver blinked, unable to believe his ears. "I go?"

"You heard me."

Peter struggled to his feet and got the door latch on his second fumbling try. Then he was behind the wheel, one hand on the ignition key, the other reaching for something out of Bolan's vision.

The Executioner saw it coming and drilled the German in the forehead before he had a chance to level the hidden automatic. Then he walked back to Monica's rental car. Her expression was solemn as she watched him through the open driver's window.

"This one needs a bath," he said.

She nodded, turned the engine over and waited for Bolan to get into the car before she inched forward, pushing the gray sedan slowly toward the brink of the pier. After another moment it toppled over, splashing out of sight.

"We've got two targets," he informed her. "You can come along, or drop me back at the hotel."

"I'm coming. Can we trust his information?"

"One way to find out."

Monica hesitated. "About my contact . . ."

"He's out of the loop," Bolan told her. "We can deal with him later. Right now we've got places to go and people to see."

8

The Lillehammer address was on the border of a residential district, facing shops across the street. There was no traffic at this hour, with the shops long closed and residents in bed or getting there. The house in question still showed lights in back, but faintly, barely visible when someone was watching from the street.

Bolan had changed en route, shedding the jacket, shirt and slacks that covered his nightsuit, slipping back into the shoulder rigging while Monica drove. He released the H&K submachine gun from its swivel mount, slotting surplus magazines into his cargo pockets.

Time.

"Six minutes starting now," Bolan said, making sure his watch was synchronized with Monica's dashboard clock.

"And then?"

"If I'm not back, you leave."

"But I—"

"No arguments," he told her firmly. "Once I wake the neighbors, they'll be calling for police. Six minutes is the maximum we can allow."

"What if something goes wrong?"

"Then I won't be coming back."

She stiffened at the tone of Bolan's voice, and that was fine. He had to get the point across in no uncertain terms.

"It's critical that one of us at least remains in play," he said. "You have your orders on Lenart, and I've got mine."

"All right."

"I mean it, Monica."

"I said all right."

He left the car and crossed the street, a gliding shadow. In his mind he was reviewing what he knew about the Einsatzgruppe from Brognola's briefing. Membership and ideology, a list of crimes suspected. Leadership.

The top guys were named Norner and Koch. He had their faces memorized for future reference, but there was little concrete information on the rank and file. A few ex-cons from Germany, but otherwise the Einsatzgruppe showed a fairly even split between the disadvantaged poor who longed for scapegoats and an upper crust of overprivileged youths who thrived on violent kicks and feared the loss of Papa's money to the creeping tide of socialism. Mix it up with a philosophy that made the youths feel special, "warriors" or a so-called "master race," and what you had was an enthusiastic kind of hatred waiting to explode.

The backyard had no gate, and Bolan edged along between two houses, moving in a combat crouch. The light that drew him on was streaming through a kitchen window at the back, illuminating a cluttered patio. He risked a glance inside and saw two young men sitting at a table, drinking beer and playing cards. A third was stooped in front of the refrigerator, checking out the stock at hand.

An easy triple, go in firing with the H&K and drop all three before they knew what was happening. No sweat.

Unless they had some backup elsewhere in the house. Unless his source had lied.

It seemed a long shot, but the captive neo-Nazi could have rattled off street numbers at random, trying to save himself. It could be mere coincidence that the address he'd given in Lillehammer was inhabited by men who fitted the Einsatzgruppe profile to a T.

The man at the refrigerator turned, a beer in hand, and Bolan saw the automatic pistol tucked into his belt. Another sweep turned up a Skorpion machine pistol on the counter, next to the stove. It was half-hidden by a cookie jar and hadn't registered on Bolan's first glance through the window.

Fair enough. Now all he had to think about was reinforcements dozing in the bedrooms, maybe sacked out in the parlor.

Never mind. A soldier could defeat himself by dwelling on the difficulties of a task, and Bolan didn't mean to let that happen here and now. He crossed the patio and checked the door, confirming that it opened inward, stepping up to land a solid kick above the knob.

The door flew open and pieces of shattered lock hurtled across the room like buckshot. Bolan followed in a rush, the MP-5K laying down a screen of cover fire, the stubby muzzle tracking in an arc from left to right across the room.

The standing Nazi never had a chance to taste his beer. A string of parabellum hollowpoints ripped through his chest, and one round burst the bottle in his hand. He hurtled backward, slammed against the door of the refrigerator, smearing it with crimson as he slithered to the floor.

His fellow Aryans gaped at the black-clad stranger, stunned and speechless, as he blew them away. One of them toppled over backward in his chair, and as he fell, a boot came up beneath the table, flipping it and spilling the cards across his playmate's corpse.

Three minutes had elapsed since he'd left the car.

He checked the living room and found it empty, turning toward the stairs when he was challenged by a startled, frightened voice. This neo-Nazi wore a pair of boxer shorts and nothing else, but he was carrying an automatic, and as Bolan turned to face him, flame erupted from the muzzle.

One round whispered past Bolan's face as he went to ground, a shoulder roll behind the nearest piece of furniture. Rounds two and three ripped through the easy chair that he'd chosen for his cover, and he knew he'd have to move or risk a hit with number four.

He came up firing and raked the staircase with a rising burst that caught the youthful fascist waist-high, spinning him around. Momentum brought him down the stairs, and Bolan finished off the magazine before his target landed at the bottom. Making sure.

He took a second to reload, then hit the stairs. Three bedrooms and a bath, all empty now.

Clean sweep.

But none of those he'd eliminated were the leaders of the gang. His source had been correct about the address, but it seemed the Lillehammer house was more an outpost than a center of command. As for the Tretten address, they would simply have to wait and see.

THE MORE SHE TRIED to tell herself she wasn't afraid, the more it bothered Monica. She knew that violent death was sometimes part and parcel of a clandestine service, but she hadn't come prepared for open warfare in the streets. It was supposed to be a relatively simple transfer, one man shifting his allegiance to the West, with Monica on hand to cope with any opposition.

Simple.

But simplicity had died at Legoland together with her Russian contact. Now, in place of one man's bid for freedom, she had neo-Nazis and a contract on her life, with the American—Belasko—bent on crippling the enemy with what he called preemptive strikes. Her own superiors were suspect, and the only person she could trust had been unknown to her the day before.

How had it happened? What was really going on behind the scenes?

"How many?" she inquired when they reached the Lillehammer outskirts, headed north toward Tretten.

"Four," Bolan said, "All muscle. No sign of the leadership."

She did some fast arithmetic. Ten dead, including those she had disposed of on the day her Russian contact had died. Assuming the Einsatzgruppe had forty men—the highest estimate, which could have been exaggerated—they were suffering from twenty-five percent attrition at the present time. It might not stop them in their tracks, but it was bound to slow them down a little.

"Do you think the three men from the restaurant will go back there?"

"I hope so," Bolan said. "They'll find homicide detectives waiting for them if they do."

But even as he spoke she knew they wouldn't be so lucky. Whether in a taxi or on foot the three survivors from the Holmenkollen restaurant would be warned off by the flashing lights of emergency vehicles. They wouldn't blunder into a potential killing situation with the odds against them.

"They'll warn the others." It was suddenly so clear that she felt like something of an imbecile for having overlooked the possibility.

"They might," Bolan replied. "It can't be helped."

"But they'll be waiting for you."

"Possibly. If anything, I tend to think they'll pack their gear and head for Lillehammer—or away. I'm more afraid of missing them than walking into any kind of trap."

She kept her eyes fixed on the road. She didn't doubt Belasko's courage or ability to fight, but she was curious about his motives. He didn't remind her of the other CIA employees she'd known since her defection to the U.S. and subsequent recruitment by the Company. It was a subtle difference, but he didn't sermonize about the Land of Opportunity or treat his mission like a game.

This man was serious, as if he bore a private grudge against the Einsatzgruppe, but he wasn't a reckless fighter, taking chances just to prove himself. She knew that he had served in Vietnam, a war she barely understood, and it was readily apparent that his war went on today.

The man was, she thought, a little like herself. Committed to a cause and willing to accept the risks involved. She only wished that she could read his mind and give that cause a proper name.

They made good time along the northbound highway. The traffic was sparse and no police cars were visible. Approaching Tretten, she was ready when her partner spread a map across his knees and started giving her directions to their target.

A commercial address this time, something like a warehouse. She noticed several cars parked on one side, and she kept going on Belasko's order, barely slowing down enough for him to check out the building.

"Looks like somebody's home," he said when they were parked a hundred yards downrange beside another dark and silent warehouse.

She had counted a half dozen cars at least. Assuming each man drove alone, Belasko would still be outnumbered six to one at a minimum.

"I want to help you."

"We've been over that," he said. "It's help enough for you to keep the engine running and your eyes wide open."

"It's *not* enough. There might be guards outside. You have no way of knowing whether there are two men in the warehouse or two dozen."

"Either way I need you here. I don't have any chance at all without an exit hatch."

"If we alerted the police..."

"And tell them what? Some men are talking in a warehouse, which they doubtless rent or own? They wouldn't even check it out unless you showed them good ID and filled them in on all the details."

He was right, of course.

"I'm going. Give me five to get inside, ten more to wrap it up. If I'm not back in fifteen minutes—"

"I go back without you," she finished for him, trying not to let the angry disappointment show.

He left without another word, the darkness covering his passage, and she felt a sudden urge to follow. Who was this Belasko to command her like a ranking officer? Perhaps he didn't trust a woman in the thick of fighting, even after she'd proved herself.

But, no. The man was a soldier who preferred to work alone. If she was with him, he'd feel compelled to watch her every move. In order to protect her, not because he thought she was incompetent.

And watching out for her could get him killed, the same way her surprise appearance on the battlefield could ruin any plans he had in mind.

Disgusted with herself, she sat behind the wheel and waited. In the dark. Alone.

THERE WERE NO GUARDS outside the warehouse. But the access doors were locked, and Bolan didn't feel like sacrificing his surprise advantage yet, before he had an opportunity to scope the layout, maybe count his enemies and see what he was up against. A ladder on the south wall of the warehouse brought him to the gently sloping roof where skylights were arranged to face the rising sun.

He moved on tiptoe, using precious time so as not to warn the men inside with any excess noise. The first skylight showed wooden crates stacked halfway to the ceiling, twelve or fifteen feet below him. Through the second Bolan had a bird's-eye view of a makeshift office, roofless, formed by the erection of partitions that were mostly glass. Six men were huddled in the office, poring over maps, while three more lounged outside on folding chairs.

Nine guns that he was sure of, and a major portion of the warehouse was beyond his view. He back-tracked to the other skylight, knowing he had no more time to waste. Glancing below to verify the drop, he cleared the skylight in a burst of automatic fire, then moved forward, stepping off into open space.

He landed in a crouch and rebounded to a shorter stack of crates. A pistol shot rang out behind him, and he flattened as a bullet sprayed his flank with splinters from the nearest crate. A gunner he'd overlooked was lining up another shot when Bolan hit him with a blazing figure eight that punched him over onto his back.

He swiveled toward the office, dropping to the concrete floor as two guns moved to intercept him. Bolan met them with a knee-high burst that dropped them both across his line of fire and finished them before they hit the floor.

Reloading on the move, he dodged into a narrow aisle between two stacks of merchandise. He had no way of knowing what the contents were and didn't care as long as they could stop incoming fire. He circled to his right, a move to flank the seven neo-Nazi gunmen still alive.

And he was halfway there when number eight came out of nowhere, dropping from the crates above directly into Bolan's path. It was dramatic, but a wise man would have used his automatic carbine from the high ground to secure a kill. Instead, he hit the floor off balance, staggered backward and was just recovering when Bolan shot him in the face.

So much for any final vestige of surprise.

He came around the corner in a slide, the MP-5K catching three of his opponents in the open, ripping them from left to right and back again. They fell together in a heap, limbs tangled, and their weapons clattered onto the floor.

Bolan scrambled to his feet, drawing the Beretta as his other adversaries doubled back in the direction of the latest firing. They were getting cautious now, a Skorpion thrust out around the corner, laying down a burst of fire that ricocheted to Bolan's left. He squeezed off two quick shots in answer, moving out before the gunner found his range and flattening against the nearest wall of packing crates.

A standoff was the last thing Bolan needed at the moment when his time was running out. It was a long walk back to Lillehammer in the blacksuit, even if he ditched his weapons to avoid immediate arrest. There was no time to waste.

He holstered the Beretta, fed the stuttergun a fresh magazine and started to climb, finding toeholds in between the crates. Twelve feet, and he was belly down on top before the Skorpion cut loose again. A longer burst this time, and Bolan wriggled forward under cover of the noise.

Beneath him the survivors were whispering, grouping themselves for a rush. He waited for a moment and let them make their break. Then he saw his opening.

It was a simple drop, the point man leading off and firing from the hip as Bolan landed just behind the stragglers. One of them sensed something, turning, but the move came too late. The MP-5K opened up at point-blank range, 9 mm parabellum rounds ripping through flesh and fabric, dropping the neo-Nazis where they stood.

The lead gun pivoted, still firing with his Skorpion, his last burst gutting the next man in line by mistake. Bolan answered with a burst that ripped the weapon from his hands and spun him like a dervish, blowing him away.

Strange faces scattered all around him, but no one who resembled Dieter Koch or Eric Norner.

Bolan spent another moment in the ringing silence, half-expecting other gunmen to emerge from hiding and continue the fight. When none appeared, he hurried toward the office, circling the desk and scooping up the map of Lillehammer that the gunners had been studying. He registered the marks in felt pen—circles, arrows—but he had no time to analyze the markings now.

Sixty-five seconds and counting before he found himself on foot.

He hit the broad doors running, leapt the steps and raced back toward the car.

The Einsatzgruppe had been cut by half, but he was still no closer to the men on top. It was a gap he'd have to close, and swiftly, if he meant to scrub their plans.

The map might help. And if it didn't he'd have to do it on his own before it was too late.

9

"How many dead?" Dieter Koch asked.

"Sixteen."

The tone of Eric Norner's voice was heavy with disgust. He shifted in his chair behind the wooden desk and glared at his subordinate across the room. It seemed to Koch that the commander of the Einsatzgruppe had nearly reached his limit.

"So? What now?"

"I'm thinking."

Sixteen dead, plus three from yesterday. Twenty-one with Fritz and Hans. More soldiers lay dead in one week's time than they'd lost in two years skirmishing with the police in France and Germany. Koch understood that something had gone seriously wrong, but he was at a loss to pin it down.

It wouldn't be police, that much was clear. When the authorities killed someone, they were prone to brag about it, trotting out their contacts in the media to film the moment for posterity. The absence of communiqués meant they were dealing with a private party...or, perhaps, an agency that chose to keep its business secret from the public.

Koch immediately thought of Jews and Communists, the Einsatzgruppe's leading enemies on earth.

He'd expected the Mossad to take an interest in their business now for months. Could it be coming true at last? The Jews were master terrorists, adept at killing those with whom they disagreed.

It was an easy thing to say, and hearing it would reinforce the nerve of his surviving soldiers, but he had no concrete proof. Whatever he decided to believe, the fact remained that enemies couldn't be beaten while they were unrecognized. In order to destroy the men responsible for so much havoc in the Einsatzgruppe ranks, Koch had to find out who they were. And so far his opponents seemed to hold a firm advantage in strategic intelligence.

"They knew exactly where to find our men."

"Some of them," Norner contradicted.

"Enough. They tricked us at the restaurant to start. It was a trap. From there—"

"I've spoken to my source again. He's concerned."

"As *we* should be. I don't think we can trust this man."

"He hasn't let us down before."

"How many failures like last night can we afford?"

The question was rhetorical, of course. They both knew that another string of killings like the ones last evening would doom the Einsatzgruppe as a fighting force. Next time the enemy might even find a way to reach the leadership.

As for the sanctity of Norner's "source," Koch had been skeptical from the beginning, weeks ago, when money and strategic information had begun to flow like manna from heaven. The stranger, who called himself Heinrich, would only meet or speak with Norner, no one else. So far his money had been good, his information accurate enough—arranging minor targets for the Einsatzgruppe to destroy—but in the light of new events it seemed entirely possible that they'd been seduced and manipulated into a position that would leave them vulnerable for a killing blow.

"Our spearhead is intact," Norner said. "Only hours now until we strike."

"And if the enemy is waiting for us?" Koch asked.

"Let him wait. What can he do against determined warriors of the master race?"

"He did enough last night."

"What's happened to your courage, Dieter? Your commitment to the cause?"

Koch stiffened in his chair. He felt the heat of anger burning in his face.

"I'm not afraid!" he snapped. "I simply don't believe in wasting everything we've worked for, all our soldiers, on a stranger's word. For all we know this friend of yours could be a Jew."

"Would any Jew have given us the blueprints to the Paris synagogue? Would he have helped us with the two Israelis in Vienna?"

"Bait," Dieter said. "Tricks to win our confidence until the time was right to bag us all at once."

Norner considered the possibility, then slowly shook his head. "The Jews are devious, I grant you, but they still protect their own. They would have seized our men in Paris and tried to make them talk. I have no doubt they would have murdered or arrested me when I agreed to meet with Heinrich."

There was logic in the man's words, but Koch wasn't convinced. Somehow someone had penetrated their security. If it hadn't been Norner's covert source, then...

"Peter."

"What?" Distracted from his private ruminations, Norner looked confused and angry.

"Peter Kroll. He was abducted from the restaurant last night and killed. The bastards could have questioned him before they shot him. Why else would they kidnap one man and leave the other three alive when they could just as easily have shot all four?"

"And Peter knew the meeting places," Norner said.

"Except for one."

"That means—" The telephone cut through his voice, and Norner mouthed a curse as he lifted the receiver.

"Yes?"

Koch saw the transformation in his comrade's face and knew it must be Heinrich calling. Norner only got that look, a sickly mixture of subservience and pride, when he was talking to the money man.

"I understand. Of course. As I was telling my associate..."

Koch wished he could hear the other man's voice, perhaps learn something from his tone and attitude. In Koch's mind the fact that Peter Kroll had likely given up his fellow warriors didn't prove that Heinrich was legitimate by any means. The ambush at the restaurant itself had been arranged, a team dispatched to kill the meddling woman on advice from Norner's wealthy "friend."

"And I agree," Norner said, nodding now, as if the caller had some way of seeing him. "That's right. Don't worry. Yes...and thank you." Hanging up the phone, the leader of the Einsatzgruppe sat back in his chair and smiled.

"The conference will proceed as planned in spite of everything."

"With more security no doubt."

"We'll cope with the security. We still have men inside, if you recall."

"Assuming they haven't been recognized and marked for death."

"Heinrich is most concerned about the incidents last night. He's investigating."

"Ah." Somehow the thought didn't put Koch at ease.

"And he has offered us ten thousand marks for each man lost."

Koch blinked. He tried to think of a retort, but how did one reject an offer of 190,000 marks? Their last three robberies combined had barely netted half of that amount.

And if he concentrated on the numbers long enough, he might forget about the cost in martyred warriors of the master race.

In war men died. It was a fact of life.

"So we proceed."

"On schedule," Norner said, and smiled.

IT HAD BEEN EASIER than Rostov had expected, fortifying Eric Norner's nerve. Like most messiahs, Norner kept his own best interest foremost in his mind, and cash meant more to any revolutionary movement—left or right—than soldiers in the field. With money in his pocket Norner could recruit new cannon fodder, arm them with the latest implements of death and turn them loose upon the world.

Or maybe not.

If things blew up in Lillehammer, Norner and his junior-league Gestapo could be hounded to their graves. Small loss for anyone outside the neo-Nazi underground, and it would save the KGB 190,000 marks.

For Rostov it would be a bargain either way.

His chief concern right now was finding out who killed the Germans in their separate lairs last night. It was a short step to surmise that someone had seen through his contact with the CIA. The setup at Holmenkollen restaurant was proof enough of that, and he wouldn't be getting back in touch with the Americans for anything. It had been helpful, while it lasted, but the link wasn't worth sacrificing all that he had worked for, his career itself.

Let the Americans chase one another now while he proceeded with the job at hand.

But if his link was compromised, what then? Was there more afoot to block his strategy and bring the whole thing crashing down around his ears?

Impossible.

His contact in the CIA hadn't been briefed on the specifics of the plan. It had been more or less a one-way street, with the Americans content to think of *perestroika* going down the drain. They were amused perhaps by the idea of Russian agents undermining the leaders at the Kremlin, but their petty games were no concern of Rostov's.

He had work to do, and at the moment it was going badly.

He had started off with thirty-seven neo-Nazis, and the fighting force had been reduced to sixteen men in four short days. Another day or two like that and they could all be gone.

But Rostov didn't need two days. If Norner's people could survive the afternoon, it would be good enough. By nine o'clock that night their work would be complete. And Rostov's triumph would be assured.

False optimism was a fatal flaw, but years of working for the KGB had taught him well enough to see beyond the moment, to extrapolate the outcome of a given plan. He could already see the headlines that would follow an assassination of the king by neo-Nazis. All of Scandinavia would rise in outrage, challenging the wisdom of a reunited Germany, and KGB provocateurs would do their part in France, Belgium, Poland, Czechoslovakia and the Netherlands. At home the Soviet government would be forced to reassess the risks of *glasnost,* taking stock of all that Mother Russia had surrendered to the West in such a short time.

And that was what he wanted, after all.

To Rostov it was unimportant whether Germany was split or reunited. He couldn't care less about the Eastern European states. What troubled him, enraged and frightened him, was standing by and watching his homeland fall apart, destroyed by "liberal" politicians with their eyes fixed on the West. Traitors like Gorbachev and Yeltsin betrayed the ideals of the people's revolution and the Communist Party, selling out their birthright for a handful of American dollars.

Soon those traitors would receive their due. He couldn't kill them all, but the politicians' loss of power was enough. They lived for influence, their egos fattened with the praise of comrades and the privileges that came with leadership. When all of that was stripped away, the bastards forced into retirement—some compelled to work like ordinary men—then Rostov's victory would be complete.

His homeland would be back on track, proceeding with the business of exporting revolution to the world at large. Accommodation with the West would be discredited, erased as fallen leaders of the government were cropped from photographs and written out of textbooks used in schools. A generation down the road no one would even know the names of Gorbachev and company and the violence they had done to Lenin's dream.

But Rostov had to take his operation one step at a time. If he should fail, if his participation in the plot should be exposed, he'd be ruined. Worse, he might be dead.

He understood that his superiors—the men who backed his scheme—would try to save themselves at any cost should things go wrong in Norway. They'd cut their losses ruthlessly, eliminating evidential links that tied them to the overall conspiracy. And Rostov knew that he'd be among the first to go.

It was a risk he'd accepted when he took the job, believing in the cause as he believed in everything he did. The torture, executions, sabotage, subversion—all of it was necessary to advance the march of socialism in a blind, resistant world. When people failed to recognize their own best interests, it was up to the enlightened few to take command and shape events. It was his duty and his privilege all in one.

Tonight, in one fell swoop, he would eliminate a crass defector and a head of state, the latter action forcing Europe to the brink of war. It didn't matter that the war would be averted by diplomacy; the very threat was victory enough for Rostov and the hard-line leaders of the KGB. This time the threat wouldn't be Russia, but the old familiar bogeymen from Auschwitz. After all these years the shadow of the swastika still haunted Europe, terrifying millions who were still unborn when Hitler's Reich had gone down in flames. It was an automatic reflex, and as such could be manipulated by a master of the game.

Tonight.

He still had calls to make, some final details to arrange, before he settled back to watch it happen. There were questions begging answers, first and foremost the identity of the assailants who were taking on the Einsatzgruppe so effectively at this least opportune of times.

For every question there must be an answer. Somewhere.

Frowning in his concentration, Rostov reached out for the telephone.

"ESCAPE ROUTES?" Monica asked.

"Looks that way," Bolan replied.

The map was spread between them on Monica's bed at the Oppland hotel. A glance had been enough to indicate the Einsatzgruppe's interest in the Rica Victoria, with arrows drawn to indicate three routes away from the hotel. The absence of incoming routes suggested that the neo-Nazis had their way inside confirmed.

"It doesn't tell us much," Monica said.

And she was right on that score. One of the escape routes doubled back to the address that Bolan had already cleared, while the other two met highways leading out of Lillehammer. There was nothing on the map to show him where the rest of Norner's gunmen could be found.

"From this," he said, "I'd say they've found a way inside."

"But how?"

"For that we'll have to take a fresh look at security. I think we can rule out a frontal assault on the hotel."

"A bomb?"

He thought about it, then finally shook his head. "For that they'd make the plant well in advance. Escape routes wouldn't enter into it. Their best shot would be putting men inside."

"The staff?"

"Could be. We don't have time to check them out across the board."

"What, then?"

"I don't suppose there's any way to scrub the conference?"

"With only hours left?" She shook her head emphatically. "That isn't possible."

"Then what we need are two additions to the guest list. You and me."

"I'm on the list already," Monica replied. "My meeting with Lenart."

"Is he supposed to make his move tonight?"

"It's open-ended. His discretion, anytime this weekend."

"Norner's people wouldn't put this kind of effort out to bag a scientist no matter where he's from. It has to be the king."

"To kill him?"

"Kill or capture, either way it means publicity."

"In spite of everything I can't believe the Company would be involved in such a thing."

"It doesn't have to be the Company, per se, just a few rogues working underground. It wouldn't be the first time."

"I feel foolish and ashamed."

"You'll have a chance to make it up," he said. "First thing, we have to deal with Norner's team."

"I'd feel better if we had some help."

"Too late. We're on our own."

It would have been a comfort to recruit some reinforcements, but the warrior knew that any call he placed through Monica's connections would be wasted, while a summons for assistance from the team at Stony Man would come too late. The morning light was breaking over Lillehammer, Friday morning coming on, and they'd truly have to do the job alone.

Say twenty members of the Einsatzgruppe were still alive, just to be on the safe side. Beyond that he could only guess at what kind of assistance Norner's people could expect from covert sponsors. Bolan hoped he wouldn't be forced to fight the CIA along with Norner's neo-Nazis, but he meant to see the mission through at any cost.

The stakes had gone beyond a mere defection now. If he was right about the move against King Harald, governmental chaos was the very least they could expect . . . and war wasn't altogether out of the question.

New stakes, right. In fact a whole new game. But one thing hadn't changed.

Mack Bolan's life was riding on the line.

10

Reinhardt Klassen stood before the full-length mirror and examined his reflection, making sure the Skorpion machine pistol wasn't visible under his jacket. The shoulder rig was perfect, and the jacket had been cut a half size larger with the specific aim of hiding weaponry. If he wasn't required to pass through any metal detectors, everything should be fine.

And with any luck at all he wouldn't even have to draw the gun.

The plan called for the "waiters" at the banquet to do all the shooting, see it finished in a moment and escape to waiting vehicles. The execution was to have been supervised by Josef Ziegler, but Ziegler had been killed attempting to abduct the woman.

Klassen would be standing in for Ziegler at the banquet, a decision made by Eric Nomor just that morning. And despite initial qualms, Klassen meant to carry off the job without a hitch.

It had been so like Ziegler, the audacious fool, to get himself killed in a ridiculous sideshow one day before the major operation, leaving Klassen to perform the job that Ziegler had prepared for all along. Examining his mirror image, Klassen noted bitterness around the mouth and eyes, adjusting his expression until any hint of dissatisfaction with his lot in life had disappeared.

There. Perfect.

None could doubt his ultimate commitment to the cause. He might be cautious—meaning he didn't plan to waste his own life or the lives of his subordinates on pointless, suicidal gestures—but he was no coward, by any means. His team had taken out the Paris synagogue last March. It had been Klassen, standing just across the street, who had keyed the detonator in his pocket and remained to film the first police arriving on the scene.

He had been brought up in a home where politics wasn't discussed. His father had lectured now and then, but that was all. He had contrived his own philosophy from what he'd picked up on the streets and what he'd seen around him day to day. It had taken him years to understand that much of what he'd learned in school had been deliberately distorted to obscure the great achievements of the National Socialists. He'd drifted through right-wing discussion groups in search of more than idle talk until he had found the Einsatzgruppe. It had been small but growing then, as yet unarmed, but that had changed. Already famous for their raids, they would be recognized as heroes one day soon.

Klassen only hoped he would survive to see the day.

And if he didn't? Many heroes—most, in fact—were only recognized in death. His sacrifice would place another sturdy brick in the foundation of a world where racial purity was paramount and Jews were swept away.

Already they'd been in touch with like-minded groups in Britain, Canada and the United States. The fire was spreading, and it didn't matter that police and the news media opposed them now. "Jewish media," one spokesman from America had called it, and the name fitted well enough. When they were stronger, once the Aryan electorate began to vote for their future instead of banking on a politician's empty promises, changes would be made.

The changes would begin tonight.

Klassen's rented room was situated a half mile from the Rica Victoria hotel. He'd driven the route several times, clocking himself, and his arrival was precisely timed for one hour before the king's appearance. His infiltrators would all be in place by that time, ready to strike at the appointed hour.

What a pity, Klassen thought, that the old king had died of natural causes before they could pick him off. It would have been poetic, a new generation of Nazis striking down the man who had resisted their forefathers in World War II. But they'd take what they could get. Tonight the king of Norway, and tomorrow... who?

Whatever the selected target, Klassen meant to be around to see it. He was mentally prepared to die, as were the other members of his troop, but that didn't suggest enthusiasm for the prospect. He wasn't some wild-eyed Muslim, after all. His death, if it came down to that, would have some greater meaning for the cause than mere blood sacrifice.

He checked the room before he left, making sure he had everything he needed for the night ahead: the gun, of course, and extra magazines; his passport and the money safely tucked away; a cyanide capsule wrapped in metal foil.

The pill was Norner's brainstorm to prevent his men from falling into hostile hands and spilling any crucial information to the enemy. By which, of course, he meant his own location and projected movements. There were times when Klassen almost questioned Eric Norner's personal devotion to the cause.

Almost.

And then he glimpsed the Führer's eyes up close and doubt dissolved.

Still, there was such a thing as going overboard.

Before he left the small apartment Klassen detoured through the bathroom, dropped his poison pill into the commode and flushed it out of sight. If he was meant to die tonight, he meant to do it like a man, a warrior.

Klassen spent another moment at the door before he left, rigging an explosive booby trap for the police. When he was done, he left the door unlocked and walked on to his car.

He was one minute early as he slid behind the wheel. The rest, he thought, would be history.

THE WORST PART, Monica Jakes thought, was trying to circumvent local security. The CIA had rightly drawn the line at sharing word of Gustave Lenart's impending defection with the Norwegians, which meant she was on her own until they reached the pickup point. At first she had expected nothing but a fine meal and some boring speeches at the conference banquet, but events within the past few days had changed all that. Now she was seeing gunmen everywhere, suspecting everyone.

She couldn't even trust the driver of the car that was supposed to lift Lenart.

The call was hers, but she was violating most, or all, of the procedures she'd learned in training with the Company. She hadn't been in touch with her control since tipping him about her nonexistent meeting at the Holmenkollen restaurant, and she was bound to raise some eyebrows by her very silence. Worse, in Langley's eyes, she was cooperating with a member of a separate, unknown agency and moving well beyond her brief to block the Einsatzgruppe's move against the conference.

In fact she had no choice.

The next time Monica touched base with her superiors she wanted contact with a senior man at Langley. Even then she would be cautious, laying out the facts and letting others draw their own conclusions from the evidence. She wouldn't risk her life again—or jeopardize her mission, risk Lenart—by acting under orders from a man who had betrayed her.

There were problems even now. The Company had helped finesse her hiring as a hostess for the banquet, and she had no way of knowing if her enemies had been informed. She might be burned well in advance before the action started, but she had no choice. The Einsatzgruppe's plot against King Harald took priority right now, preventing her from scrubbing her agreement with Lenart and lifting him ahead of time. The banquet had to proceed on schedule, and they'd have to take the action as it came.

Her long gown hid the Walther automatic taped against her inner thigh. It would be awkward and a bit embarrassing to draw the weapon, but she had no other ready hiding place. And when the shooting started, no one would be looking at the hostess, anyway.

At least she hoped not.

If the Einsatzgruppe had her covered . . .

Guests were filing in now, some with wives, all dressed in formal wear. The hostesses took turns escorting them to preselected tables, Monica deliberately stalling for the chance to seat Lenart. He was surprised to see her, but he covered well and followed her across the room.

"If there's any trouble, slide beneath your table instantly," she told him. "You understand?"

"What kind of trouble?"

"Don't try to reach the exit. That's very important."

"All right."

He was the first guest seated at his table, and she noticed that his hands were trembling as he tucked them out of sight.

"I'll be close by," she assured him. "You have friends here."

His smile was feeble, but at least he managed. From her own defection years before Monica understood his feelings, the internal conflict. He was leaving home, the only life he had ever known, and now he faced the risk of being murdered for his trouble. Months of planning the move couldn't eliminate anxiety on the appointed day.

She moved back toward the entrance of the banquet chamber and seated other guests, exchanging smiles with staff and scientists alike. She scanned the faces of the waitresses and waiters, wishing photos of the Einsatzgruppe soldiers had been made available for her to memorize.

Too late.

Besides Lenart the one familiar face so far was Mike Belasko's. She'd seen him briefly in the lobby, coming in, but he had disappeared. It was too late for him to find a place among the waiters, but she hoped he'd be close at hand.

The king had already arrived, his limousine and motorcade unloading in the hotel's porte cochere. He traveled with security, of course—and they were clearly on alert—but to her certain knowledge no one had informed His Majesty of the immediate, impending danger. She could only hope his men would be alert.

And what if they mistook Belasko and herself for enemies? It was the first time she had given any conscious thought to being shot down by the very men she'd come to help. Another risk that she'd have to cope with in the deadly game.

The banquet hall was filling up. There were still twenty minutes left before the conference would officially begin, but everyone was anxious to see new faces and old friends. Some of the delegates were circulating, slapping backs and shaking hands. The room hummed with conversation, glasses clinking as the early rounds of wine were served.

Ten minutes.

Leaders of the conference were filing out across the dais, several standing by their seats while others broke off into groups and talked among themselves. An air of anticipation communicated itself to the others, conversation lagging as the delegates began to drift back to their seats.

It was chilling to think of the killers already in place, waiting for the opportunity to strike. Would they be members of the hotel staff? Perhaps a delegate or two among the lot? Or did they have some other scheme in mind?

She wished they could simply get the waiting part behind them, face whatever dangers would arise and see it finished. She was getting nervous, marking time and faking smiles when she felt more like venting her frustration in a scream.

She picked out two men from the king's security detachment in the banquet hall and knew there had to be more outside. A momentary hope flashed through her mind that they'd stop the Einsatzgruppe on their own without the need for any bloodshed in the dining room itself, but Monica already knew the odds of that were slim to none.

The neo-Nazis had a way inside. She knew it with a certainty that she couldn't have verbally explained. Almost an intuition, if she had believed in such things.

There was danger close at hand, perhaps within her reach, and she could do nothing to head it off.

On the dais one of the conference VIPs was tapping his butter knife against an empty wineglass, signaling his colleagues to be seated.

She found herself a corner near the entrance, waiting, conscious of the pistol pressed against her inner thigh. Its weight was somewhat less than reassuring in the circumstances.

Then there was silence in the dining hall as the master of ceremonies prepared to introduce his royal guest of honor

Soon now

MACK BOLAN ENTERED through the kitchen, flashing false security credentials, moving past the chefs and helpers who were putting the finishing touches on a course of appetizers. No one seemed to notice him or care that he was there as long as he stayed out of their way. He made it to the entrance of the banquet hall, glanced through the door and found himself staring at the back of a genuine royal security guard.

His bogus credentials were fair quality, but there was no way he could pass inspection by a member of the king's own guard, much less respond to an interrogation in Norwegian.

It was down to choices now. He could attempt to drop the guard himself and risk a public scene, or he could wait. The second course of action held less immediate risk, but it also would delay his entry when— not if—the fighting started.

Choices.

Bolan unbuttoned his jacket, granting easy access to the MP-5K on its swivel sling. The extra magazines were tucked inside his belt, but he'd have to watch himself from this point on. Undisciplined fire inside the dining hall would be disastrous, but his enemies would have no such restrictions on their own approach. If anything, the Einsatzgruppe commandos would be looking for inflated body counts.

He heard a ripple of applause, quickly spreading, and risked another glance through the door. King Harald was on the dais now, approaching his empty seat with one hand raised to acknowledge a standing ovation. A bright smile lit the monarch's face. If he had any notion of the danger he was facing at that moment, he gave no sign.

The introductions were completed in another moment, scattered applause dying away as the king stood before the speaker's podium. The monarch offered greetings in his native tongue, then switched to English as the language most likely to be understood by a majority of the assembled delegates.

"Good evening and welcome to Oslo, esteemed members of the world scientific community. It is my great pleasure..."

Bolan tuned out the rest, risking another glance through the door as a waitress breezed through. The security guard had shifted position, moving closer to the dais as the king began his speech. A few more yards and Bolan might be able to—

It started suddenly, a waiter moving toward the kitchen hesitating in midstride behind the security guard, thrusting a hand inside his short jacket at the same moment. Bolan caught the movement from the corner of his eye, already swiveling in that direction as the gun came into view.

It was an automatic with a silencer attached, extended in a single, fluid motion, sliding out to skin-touch range behind the security man's left ear. King Harald's voice drowned out the muffled shot, but Bolan saw it strike, a burst of gray and crimson as the guard pitched forward onto his face.

Across the banquet hall he had a glimpse of other waiters hesitating, dropping towels or trays and bringing weapons into view. There was no sight of Monica from where he stood, but Bolan had to move, and quickly, with the nearest gunner swinging toward the dais now.

He shouldered through the swing door as someone started shouting in the audience, a security officer throwing himself across the dais and tackling the king where he stood. The nearest gunman had his back to Bolan, lining up a shot and pausing for a heartbeat as the king dropped below his line of fire.

It was the break that Bolan needed, and he swung his submachine gun into target acquisition as he squeezed the trigger, stitching five rounds up the gunner's spine between his waist and shoulder blades. The sudden impact drove his target toward the dais, sprawling inches short of contact with the table.

Delegates were spilling from their seats now, scattering for cover as the other waiters opened fire. Bolan saw a second security agent go down, and then a third, both caught off guard by the sudden explosion of violence.

On the far side of the room one agent had a pistol in his hand, and he got off a single shot before another neo-Nazi in disguise caught him from behind, squeezing off two rounds from point-blank range.

How many guns? Bolan dodged behind an empty table, tipping it for cover, making a rapid scan of the room as he did so. Monica was visible now, crouching near the entrance with a pistol in her hand, and Bolan picked out four assassins he was sure of, possibly another one or two already ducking out of sight.

Fair odds in any other situation, but his fire zone was restricted by the running, dodging delegates. A few more moments and the king's own reinforcements would arrive, intent on any stranger spotted with a gun.

The doomsday numbers, right.

He pushed off from his hiding place and started for the dais, running in a combat crouch.

11

Despite her alertness Monica came close to missing the start of the battle. She was glancing to her left, watching two waiters in muted conversation, when a sudden movement near the dais caught her eye. She swung around in that direction just in time to see one of the king's security agents drop to the floor with arms outflung. Behind him one of the uniformed waiters was brandishing a pistol, turning toward the speaker's podium.

And then all hell broke loose.

She ripped the skirt of her gown, lunging for the Walther in its hidden sheath, but she could never hope to drop the gunman with a shot from where she stood. As if on cue, she saw Belasko lunging from the kitchen with his submachine gun spitting flame, the sudden sound of gunfire shocking everyone into momentary silence.

Before the screams began.

She swiveled toward the nearest waiters with her pistol cocked and leveled just in time to see them breaking for the nearest exit, looking terrified. Confused, she let them go and swept her gaze around the banquet hall, noting several other "waiters" who had stood their ground, producing guns from underneath their jackets.

Clearly only some of the serving staff were Einsatz-gruppe plants, but she could pick out four or five from where she stood. The nearest of the lot was fifty feet away and moving toward the dais with an automatic pistol in his fist. One of the delegates collided with the gunman, and she saw the neo-Nazi shove him roughly backward, squeezing off a shot that struck the scientist dead-center in his chest.

She took off in pursuit, the long skirt whipping at her legs, slowing her down. The gunman must have seen her coming, for he spun to face her, squeezing off a quick shot on the move. She dodged and heard the bullet whisper past her, hesitating for an instant longer to confirm her aim before she squeezed the trigger.

She got off two rounds at a range of twenty feet, and they were both on target, ripping through her adversary's chest and stomach. Stunning impact punched him sprawling backward on the carpet, and his last shot was directed at the ceiling, wasted.

She had no clear view of Belasko now, and she could only hope he had gone to ground, maneuvering for position on their surviving enemies. If he was hit already...

Monica blanked her mind to the grim possibility, concentrating on her own next target as the firing spread. There were six rounds left in her Walther, and she paused beside the body of the gunman she had killed, scooping up his weapon with the silencer attached.

It was a Baretta, identical to the one she'd given Belasko. Two rounds were gone, which meant she had at least thirteen remaining—one more if the Einsatz-gruppe assassin kept a live round in the chamber and a full magazine.

A group of conference delegates rushed toward her, saw the pistols she carried and reversed directions, running toward another exit. Monica was focused on the other gunmen now, at least four dressed as waiters, but she couldn't overlook the possibility that one or more might be disguised as members of the scientific gathering. That meant there were only three men in the dining hall that she could trust: the king, Belasko and Gustave Lenart.

Where *was* Lenart?

She hadn't paid particular attention to him since he'd taken his seat, and now she couldn't pick him out in the confusion. Monica hoped he had heeded her advice and taken cover at the first sign of danger, but even crawling underneath a table wouldn't guarantee his safety in the middle of a free-fire zone.

There was a scuffling at the nearest exit, thirty paces distant, and she saw a pair of royal security agents fighting to force their way inside, hampered by the crush of diners trying to escape. One of the Einsatz-gruppe "waiters" sprayed the doorway with a compact machine pistol, dropping several of the scientists, ducking and weaving when the royal guards tried to return fire.

Monica fired a shot on the move, trusting the familiar PPK, and winged him. Staggering, the gunman didn't seem to comprehend his danger, firing another long burst toward the exit jammed with bodies. More delegates fell, and Monica saw one of the security guards go down before she squeezed off two more rounds and dropped the shooter onto his face.

It was a contest now for decibels between the shouts and gunfire. Men were cursing, several crying out in pain or fear, while several female guests were screaming their lungs out, like contestants for auditions in a horror film. Some of the Einsatzgruppe gunmen—like the first one she had killed—had come equipped with silenced weapons, and she had to pick them out by sight, the swirls and eddies in the panicked crowd when one of them stood up and opened fire.

She saw at least two firing toward the dais, no doubt trying for the king, and Monica could only pray he was safely out of range. The sound of automatic fire ripped through the babel, but Monica ignored it, concentrating on the visual as she moved toward the stage.

It would be something of a miracle, she realized, if anyone emerged unscathed from the chaotic action. She was just as likely to be shot by royal security as by the neo-Nazis, but she dared not hesitate.

The waiting all came down to this—a job of do-or-die. And she was honor-bound to do. Until she died.

REINHARDT KLASSEN loitered around the Rica Victoria's gift shop, perusing pewter figurines and Nordic knitwear while the banquet guests filed in and took their seats. It seemed to take forever, waiting for the doors to close with solemn guards outside. Two men were stationed at the exit nearest the point where Klassen stood, but they dismissed him with a glance. Another tourist looking for the perfect souvenir to buy for friends or family.

The ripple of applause was muted, but he heard it all the same. It quickened Klassen's pulse, and he imagined his commandos taking their positions, drawing weapons as the king approached the podium. By that time Klassen had his Skorpion in hand, concealed beneath a heavy sweater he'd lifted from the nearest rack.

He moved back toward the cashier's counter, veering at the final instant, noting a look of mild consternation on the saleswoman's face. Shoplifting was unknown at the Rica Victoria, and he could almost hear her fabricating explanations for the tourist's strange behavior.

Nothing she could think of would prepare her for what happened next as Klassen started firing through the sweater, catching the two security agents off guard and dropping them both into a heap. Moving swiftly now, he tossed the smoldering sweater aside and crossed to the entrance, stepping through into a scene of chaos.

King Harald was no longer visible on the dais, and Klassen felt a momentary surge of elation, hoping the first rounds had scored an early kill. The rest would just be getting out alive. No simple task, but neither was it insurmountable when your commandos were expendable.

There was more gunfire near the dais, at the far end of the room from where he stood. On Klassen's right, some eighty feet away, he saw a dark man in a suit rise up from cover, firing with a stubby automatic weapon, and a member of the Einsatzgruppe went down.

Security?

This tall man didn't fit the mold of royal guards, nor was his suit exactly right. But, then, who could he be?

At once it clicked in Klassen's mind. The enemy who had been raiding Einsatzgruppe hideouts and disrupting operations for the past two days. They'd gone looking for a woman, but his chauvinistic mind dictated there had to be a man behind the scenes.

And here he was.

Klassen made up his mind and struck off through the crush of milling bodies toward his chosen target. His commandos were already coping with royal security in fine style, spraying the dais with searching fire when they had a chance. Klassen was left to eliminate the one immediate threat to their ultimate triumph.

Preoccupied with following the stranger, Klassen stumbled on the prostrate body of a wounded man, evoking painful groans before he found his balance and proceeded on his way. A running woman jostled Klassen, and she gave a startled yelp of pain as he struck her with the Skorpion, knocking her aside.

And suddenly he lost his target in the sea of bobbing heads and weaving bodies. There! And gone again. He saw one of the Einsatzgruppe's "waiters" breaking toward the dais, scrambling across a capsized table with his gun in hand, but then a burst of automatic fire from somewhere on the floor caught up with him and dropped him like a sack of laundry onto the stage.

The dark man striking back again.

Klassen lashed out with his weapon in a chopping motion, opening the bald scalp of a conference delegate too slow in stepping aside. A shocked woman saw the gun aimed at her face and fainted dead away, obstructing Klassen's path. He felt a sudden urge to kill her but he needed to conserve his ammunition for the enemy.

As if in answer to his thoughts, the stranger rose from cover, tracking with his automatic weapon, dark eyes locking onto Klassen's in a heartbeat. They were face-to-face at fifteen yards, with panicked men and women milling in the way.

The stranger hesitated, visibly reluctant to injure civilians, but Klassen felt no such compunction. He leveled the Skorpion and squeezed off a sweeping burst from left to right and back again, the bodies toppling or taking flight. It was working, but it cost him, and he had to feed the Skorpion a fresh magazine before he could continue the attack. By that time his elusive target had sidestepped and dropped out of sight behind another upturned table.

Never mind.

The Skorpion was loaded with steel-jacketed loads for maximum penetration, allowing for furniture, podiums and walls of average thickness when the strike went down.

He saw an opening and hosed the table with a looping burst, spraying jagged shards of wood in all directions. Anyone behind that table was as good as dead unless . . .

The dark man came up firing from a point ten feet on Klassen's left, the muzzle-flash of his submachine gun riveting Klassen's gaze like a strobe light. Klassen was aware of firing back, perhaps a hit, but he was taking hits himself, stiff body blows that drove him backward, off his feet and over onto his back.

There should have been more pain, all things considered. He was dying obviously, but the long-anticipated agony didn't kick in. Instead, a kind of glacial numbness radiated from the center of his chest and downward, paralyzing everything below the waist. His arms were mobile, but the Skorpion had skittered out of reach when he went down.

A shadow blocked the ceiling lights from shining in his eyes, and Klassen recognized his mortal enemy in silhouette. The man knelt down beside him, reaching out to check the pulse in Klassen's neck before he asked, "How many men? Where are they?"

Klassen summoned up his best contemptuous expression.

"Fuck you, American." And then the world went black for the Aryan superman.

THERE WERE THREE GUNNERS left that Bolan could identify, and he was on another of them even as he left the well-dressed shooter lifeless on the floor. Moving out, he fed the H&K its final surplus magazine and hoped it would be enough. He still had the Beretta to fall back on, but he liked to keep an edge if possible.

The nearest target was surrounded by a swirl of running delegates, his pistol pointed at the ceiling for a moment, snapping down in the direction of the silent daio once the line of fire was clear. As Bolan watched, he fired two shots directly at the podium, two more immediately to the left, for grazing fire beneath one of the banquet tables.

Bolan took a chance and capped him with a 3-round burst of almost surgical precision, taking off the right side of the gunner's face and dropping him before he had a chance to fire again. Blood sprayed a woman ducking past the gunner when he died, evoking sudden nausea that brought her to her knees.

How many left?

Two gunners were visible, and the possibility of reinforcements standing by outside the banquet hall or in the hotel car parks couldn't be ruled out. Time was clearly running out until one of the Einsatzgruppe guns pulled off a lucky shot.

Bolan leapt across a fallen chair and hit the carpet running toward his next selected target. The gunman's survival sense must have warned him, for he was turning now, swinging his Walther P-38 with its bulky suppressor toward the new, threatening target.

He got one shot off, plucking Bolan's sleeve, before the little H&K stuttergun kicked in with a hot figure eight. Bolan's human target did a jerky little dance, his jacket popping from the impact of killing rounds.

How many rounds remained in the submachine gun? With the weapon's cyclic rate it was impossible to count with any kind of accuracy. He'd have to pull the magazine to check, and that would leave him open to attack while he secured his hardware.

Screw it. He'd go with what he had and do his best to stay alive.

One gunner was still in motion, clubbing scattered diners as he bulled his way directly toward the speaker's podium. From the expression on the neo-Nazi's face he knew which way the wind was blowing, and he meant to carry off his mission even if it meant his own certain death.

Bolan struck off through the crush on a collision course, desperate to intercept the Einsatzgruppe thug before he reached the dais with its stock of VIPs. He sidestepped a kneeling woman, rolled across a table where the china lay in shattered ruins and came out of the roll in a fighting crouch. The gunman saw his opposition now, but he'd already committed himself to the jump.

They fired together, muzzle-flashes ten or fifteen feet apart. The rising burst from Bolan's submachine gun caught his target in the abdomen and ripped across his chest, tumbling him end over end in flight. The neo-Nazi's first round missed completely, but his second traced a line of fire along the curve of Bolan's ribs beneath his left arm. He stood his ground, unflinching, while the airborne Aryan collided with the speaker's podium and brought it down.

A sudden, almost eerie calm descended on the banquet hall, anguished voices faltering and falling off entirely once the stimulus of gunfire was removed. Across the room he noted men and women rising from their places on the floor, peering cautiously around the room beneath a drifting pall of gunsmoke. Apprehensive eyes met Bolan's, others shifting to the far side of the room where Monica was standing with a pistol in each hand, but when the firing didn't resume, they gradually decided the crisis was past.

On the dais King Harald was being helped to his feet by two of the conference leaders who solicitously brushed dust and lint from his expensive suit. The king looked dismayed, but he recovered swiftly, concern for others instantly replacing momentary fear as he beheld the carnage in the banquet hall.

They had to move before surviving members of the royal security force recovered from initial shock. Bolan moved across the dining hall with loping strides, reached Monica and took her by the arm.

"We're out of time!" he snapped.

"Lenart?"

"Where is he?"

"I don't know. I lost sight of him when the shooting started."

"Dammit! If we hang around to look for him, we're screwed."

"I can't just leave him here. He might be hurt."

They had to reach a compromise without delay.

"All right," Bolan said, "let me have your weapon and I'm out of here. Do whatever it is a hostess does at times like this, but watch your back."

"I will."

He left her to it, Monica detaining him just long enough to plant a quick kiss on his cheek. Outside the banquet hall he merged with numbers of the curious who filled the lobby, waiting for police and fresh security detachments to arrive.

He barely noticed them as he retreated toward the street and his rental car. His mind was filled with arithmetic, subtracting lifeless neo-Nazis from the working total of the Einsatzgruppe membership.

He had dealt with three gunners on his own, say seven overall to keep it on the safe side. If the forty-soldier estimate was accurate, that left a dozen brownshirts, give or take, in fighting trim.

Somewhere. But where?

He had to find them soon. And if he failed?

A frown carved furrows in the warrior's face. In that case he was fairly sure the remnants of the Einsatzgruppe would find him.

12

Eric Norner slammed down the telephone receiver with force enough to crack the plastic. For a moment he was tempted to rip the instrument out of the wall and fling it across his makeshift office, but he restrained himself with supreme effort.

"Goddamn!" he roared.

Dieter Koch was reluctant to speak, but he had to find out what had thrown Norner into such a rage. "What is it?"

"Disaster," Norner muttered. "Seven soldiers dead, including Klassen. If the early news is accurate, they missed the king."

Koch felt as if a solid blow had been delivered to his chest above his heart. He had to remind himself consciously to breathe. "All dead?"

"The drivers got away, but no one from the spearhead made it out of the hotel. The police are making an announcement for television in an hour or so."

"We have to leave," Koch said, "before it's too late."

"Too late?" The tone of Norner's voice was mocking, harsh. "You think we haven't already passed the point of no return?"

"We still have soldiers left, and the publicity from this attempt—despite its failure—will ensure us new recruits. We can rebuild within a year or eighteen months and try another plan."

"Of course. And what about my promise to our sponsors, Dieter? Are you expecting them to shrug and walk away?"

"What can they do?" Koch asked. "Inform the police? They share responsibility for everything that's happened up to now. I think they would be relieved to see it end."

"Well, think again," Norner snapped. "They expect delivery on a promise once the money's been paid . . . and spent."

"If necessary we can pay them back," Koch said. "A bank or two when the heat dies down."

"They don't want the money, Dieter! It's the king they want, and nothing else. These men don't bargain for a consolation prize."

"What then?"

"We must fulfill our contract, or a new one will be put out . . . on us."

Koch kept his face deliberately blank. He didn't know their sponsors—that was Norner's business—but he understood their reputation for ruthless efficiency. He didn't wish to start a new war with numerically superior enemies just now, when sixty percent of the Einsatzgruppe's fighting force was lying dead on mortuary slabs.

"The king?" he asked.

"Perhaps." The frown on Norner's face was thoughtful now. "I might be able to negotiate a slight revision in the contract on the basis of depleted strength. Perhaps a secondary target."

"Do you think so?"

"I can only ask. If they're not amenable . . ."

"Then we'll do the job ourselves if necessary. Blood and honor."

Even though the words rang hollowly in his mind, they had an obvious impact on Norner. The leader of the Einsatzgruppe stiffened in his chair, squared his shoulders and stared at his second-in-command.

Brand-new energy infused Norner where he sat, stiffening his resolve as it had his spine. A fresh defiance was reflected in his red-rimmed eyes, and Koch could almost see him going out to stalk the king alone.

Almost.

But hunting targets in the street was never Norner's style. He had his troops for that while he remained behind the lines and formulated strategy for other men to carry out. It was a mark—and burden—of leadership.

"How will you tell them?" Koch inquired.

"I won't have to," Norner said. "By now they know."

And that made sense, of course. With all the cash their sponsors had expended on the Lillehammer plot, it stood to reason that observers would be on the scene, confirming that they got their money's worth. At once a question surfaced in his mind: would the anonymous sponsors even give the Einsatzgruppe another chance, or would they simply pull the plug and start again from the beginning, wiping out their deadwood in the process?

No.

He couldn't make himself believe that they were marked for death. Not yet. There must be *something* they could do to make it right.

The telephone began to jangle stridently. Across the desk Norner turned to face the instrument with an expression of the darkest loathing on his face. It rang three times before he lifted the receiver to his face. "Hello?"

The change on Norner's face told Koch who the caller was—the secret sponsor who would only speak to Norner on the telephone since the initial meeting months before. Bad news traveled fast, indeed.

"I'm doing everything I can," Norner said, flushing crimson from the collar up. "Of course I understand. I'll wait to hear from you. All right."

He cradled the receiver. The angry color had drained from his face for the most part, and Norner seemed exhausted as he raised his eyes to meet Koch's gaze.

"What now?"

"He has another target for us," Norner replied. "As he says, 'An opportunity to make things right.'"

"Another target? Where? Who is it?"

"We'll be told in time. Meanwhile, we wait."

INCREDIBLY Gustave Lenart had come through the fiasco in the banquet hall without a major injury. One shoulder and his shin were bruised, where others had collided with him in the panic to escape, but he had followed the instructions of his contact, dropping beneath his table when the shooting started.

How on earth could she have known?

The wonder of it was that no one had appeared to fire on *him*. From all he had heard, the little he had seen, it was apparently an effort to assassinate the king.

Coincidence.

How could the killers even know he existed? They were caught up in their own conspiracy, too busy to concern themselves with Czech physicists who sought a different life-style in the West. The men who murdered monarchs didn't bother to concern themselves with peasants.

Still . . .

How did his contact happen to predict a violent outbreak at the banquet? Was she simply being cautious, or had she expected the attack?

More to the point, was she expecting something else? Perhaps an effort to assassinate Lenart?

He smiled and shook his head. "Assassination" was a term reserved for royalty and government officials. If and when Lenart was killed, it would be plain and simple murder. "Liquidation," in the language of the KGB.

Lenart had known there might be efforts to dissuade him from defecting, even physical attempts to bring him back, but would the Soviets really kill him? According to the new, improved government, those days were gone forever. Liberty and human rights had triumphed, beating down the KGB and those who would shackle democracy.

He knew more than ever that he wouldn't be safe until he set foot in the States. Gustave Lenart wasn't significant enough to rate a transatlantic contract on his life. Few men, in fact, would qualify in that respect, and he wasn't among their number.

Thankfully.

The problem now was waiting for his contact to get back in touch, for someone to inform him what would happen with the conference.

Several of the delegates were dead or injured. He'd seen them lying on the carpet, going out on stretchers when the shooting finally stopped and he was able to evacuate the room. There had been no sign of his contact then, although she'd been present moments earlier when it began.

A sudden fear gripped Lenart's mind. Suppose she'd been wounded, even killed? What then? How could he manage the defection on his own?

With courage, if it came to that.

Whatever happened now, within the next few hours or days, he wasn't going back to Moscow or his own country, not even if it meant his life.

He knew a number of other physicists now present at the conference, two or three of them from England. He could check to make sure they were safe, approach them quietly and ask for help. In that respect the chaos that had resulted from the shooting might be helpful, like a blessing in disguise. Police would certainly be in and out of the hotel for hours, making hostile interference with another guest unlikely.

But he couldn't—wouldn't—make the move until he gave his contact from America a chance. He found it difficult to think of her as an American, knowing as he did that she was a Czech and a defector like himself. The difference was that she had made it on her own in harder times, outwitting both the STB and KGB by sheer determination.

She inspired him with her courage, giving him the will to stand his ground, but he was frightened that she might now be a casualty of the attack upon King Harald. Their arrangement didn't call for him to get in touch with her directly, though he had a number he could call to leave a coded message in case of emergency.

His hand was resting on the telephone receiver when he stopped himself. Not yet. He didn't wish to push the panic button when, for all he knew, there might be nothing wrong. The fact of an attempt upon the king didn't prevent his own planned defection from proceeding on schedule.

Still, it troubled Lenart to think of breaking in another contact at this point in the proceedings. He wasn't a superstitious man, but luck was relative, and she'd brought him this far. If she couldn't help him the rest of the way...

The phone rang then, its sudden noise making Lenart jump, the vibration causing him to jerk his hand away in reflex action. He felt foolish. He must look like a scared old woman, standing here alone and trembling.

"Yes?"

"You recognize my voice?"

Immediate relief. She was alive and sounded fit enough. His legs folded as if on command, and he sat down on the bed. "I do."

"Is everything all right?"

"I think so. Yes."

"You weren't injured?"

"No. I'm fine."

"Tonight, then, while we have the chance. Are you prepared?"

"I am."

"The park. Eleven-thirty?"

"Yes, I'll be there."

Hanging up the phone, Lenart felt new and unexpected energy flow through his body. It was happening! His dream was coming true! Another ninety minutes and he'd be on his way to freedom in the West.

He changed clothes quickly, dressing for warmth and comfort. He'd leave the suits and other things behind. A bag would be conspicuous, and he was ready with a story of a midnight stroll to let his nerves unwind if anyone should question him as he was leaving the hotel.

An hour and a half.

It seemed like nothing when he mouthed the words, but he was wise enough to know how time could drag. Those ninety minutes would feel like ninety days before he met his contact and her driver picked them up.

They had a slogan in the West: today is the first day of the rest of your life. Lenart could only hope it wouldn't be the last.

For Alexandrei Rostov his last call of the night was almost an afterthought. Simple housecleaning, an attention to detail that had placed him where he was today.

And where, he asked himself with a degree of irony, was that?

The plan hadn't exactly blown up in his face. The king was still alive, but that was secondary to the volume of publicity that would result once his assailants were identified as members of the Einsatzgruppe. And he still had neo-Nazis in reserve, enough to stage another incident or two if necessary to keep the ball rolling.

He'd sensed the fear in Eric Norner's voice, but Norner was a realist. The neo-Nazi understood that he wouldn't last long without financial aid and the material support his nameless sponsors could provide. The Einsatzgruppe was badly wounded, but it wasn't dead. Not yet. And Norner would do everything he could to keep the movement viable, since he was nothing in the absence of his followers.

They were pathetic bastards, posing in their uniforms for private snapshots, gathering in basements to discuss their paranoid image of the New World Order. Hitler had begun his march to power much the same, but he'd been a man of twisted vision, sick charisma, whereas Norner and his handful of disciples never rose above the level of vicious school-yard bullies.

They were idiots, but at the moment they were *useful* idiots. He might find other work for them to do, another chance to strike while the iron was hot and validate the European fears of a resurgence of the Nazi underground.

Why not?

Disinformation was a useful tool, and if you had some real live neo-Nazis to exploit, so much the better. It gave the public and the politicians something they could focus on, a concrete menace far removed from Moscow and the KGB.

Meanwhile, at home, the specter of a Nazi renaissance—however far away or improbable it seemed— would spark emotional reactions in a nation that remembered Leningrad, the thousands of atrocities and countless wasted lives.

Forgetfulness wasn't a Russian trait. Forgiveness was reserved for priests.

He tapped the final number out from memory and got an answer on the first ring.

"Yes?"

"Did you enjoy the entertainment?"

"It was different."

Rostov smiled. It was a treat to meet a killer with a sense of humor.

"Are you ready to proceed?"

"I am."

"Tonight, then. Wait for the police to leave. You shouldn't have to risk yourself."

"It shall be done."

There was nothing more to say, and Rostov replaced the handset in its cradle, resting his elbows on the desk and making a steeple of his fingertips.

More wheels in motion, an elaborate machine that worked around the clock, consuming lives, converting them to energy, excreting rubble in its wake. Sometimes he saw the Party as a kind of mechanism, built to serve the people's revolution. A machine needed fuel and lubrication, all the more if it was operating every moment, every day, year-round.

The fuel for Rostov's war machine was raw imagination, and the lubricant was blood. Its driving energy was one part fear and one part dedication, inextricably entwined.

Men served the Party out of loyalty. Loyalty was procured by education, with a system of rewards and punishment to drive the sacred message home. Without that discipline the Party message would be wasted, precious words of wisdom scattered to a heedless wind.

When Rostov joined the KGB at twenty years of age, he had believed he could serve the revolution best by weeding out its enemies. He still believed that basic truth, but he had also learned that sometimes it was necessary to create those enemies before you tracked them down, exposed them to the masses and began to mete out punishment.

The years of relative peace had softened Mother Russia. Even with Afghanistan the danger had been far away and screened by censorship, as much removed from the realities of Ivan in the street as combat on the moon or Mars. Before the nation could unite and halt its suicidal drift toward Western decadence, the people needed enemies to teach them fear.

And it was Rostov's job to drive the lesson home, a task he looked forward to with relish.

13

Vasily Kirov sipped his glass of wine and watched the elevators, waiting. One advantage of the Rica Victoria's cocktail lounge was an unobstructed view of the lobby. When his target surfaced, he'd be prepared.

The pistol Kirov wore beneath his sport coat was a .22-caliber semiauto with a factory-installed suppressor. It was an assassin's weapon, virtually silent with the proper ammunition, accurate enough to score consistent killing hits at any range below fifty feet. For ammunition he'd chosen subsonic hollowpoints, projectiles that would mushroom to the size of a dime on contact with human flesh and bone, producing lethal hydrostatic shock.

Kirov wouldn't be making the kill at anything close to his weapon's maximum range. In fact, he planned to make the shot at skin-touch range, where he could look his human target in the eye and watch the fear take hold.

It was among the things that Kirov most enjoyed about his job—the power just before the kill.

The call had come as a relief. After the eruption at the banquet, he'd been concerned that he might not be needed, after all. In the confusion it would be a simple thing to spend an extra bullet on Lenart and have it done.

The job would fall to Kirov now, and that was fine. He was prepared. In fact he'd been gravely disappointed at the thought of going home again without a chance to kill. The private opportunities in Moscow were few and far between these days. Danger was a part of the reward to some degree, but he'd gotten used to knowing he wouldn't be arrested for his crimes. The thought of prison and the things that sometimes happened to a man of sensitivity behind stone walls made Kirov's blood run cold.

The risk was minimal tonight, however, with police preoccupied by the events surrounding the abortive banquet. There were dead and wounded to be taken care of, gunmen to identify, accomplices to search for in the streets. A guard was mounted at the Rica Victoria in case the villains returned, but Kirov knew there was little chance of that.

By this time the survivors would be burrowed deeply underground or on their way for parts unknown, intent on salvaging what they could from the situation. Kirov hoped they'd been paid well, considering the losses they'd taken.

And to no result.

The king was still alive. For all the gunmen had accomplished, they might as well have opened fire on the public street, shooting strangers at random. Even so he understood that terrorists thrived on publicity, oftentimes judging the success of a mission more by the headlines it reaped than the actual body count.

Unlike himself.

Kirov's was a private pleasure, closely guarded. He had no use whatsoever for publicity. The very thought unnerved him. If his game was ever exposed...

Not likely.

He'd picked the winning team, and minor setbacks in the realm of politics were transitory. Kirov had time and history on his side.

The elevator doors slid open, and Gustave Lenart emerged. He glanced around, as if expecting company, then started for the exit.

Time.

Kirov finished his wine and reached beneath his sport coat to adjust the shoulder holster, then slid off his bar stool. He took his time. There was no point in rushing now and risking premature disclosure.

He had time. Lenart couldn't outrun him now.

A simple midnight stroll perhaps. At least Lenart would try to make it look that way. In fact he could be meeting with his contact anytime now to arrange the break.

Or not.

It made no difference whatsoever to Kirov, one way or the other. He was being paid to kill Lenart on cue, and the order had been received. It didn't matter now if Lenart went ahead with his defection plan or not. His fate was sealed, and there was no way on earth for him to secure a reprieve.

The night was cool outside, not bitterly cold like winter, but there were no such things as steamy nights this close to the Arctic Circle. Kirov's jacket cut the chill enough to keep him comfortable, and he had a growing fire inside to keep him warm.

Emerging from the hotel lobby to the porte cochere, he glanced left and right in turn. Lenart was on his left, a half block distant, disappearing into the shadow as he left the hotel lights behind. He didn't glance around to see if he was being followed, trusting fate or pure dumb luck to keep him safe.

This time it wouldn't be enough.

Kirov fell in step behind his target, picking up the pace a little just to keep Lenart in sight. His shoes were rubber-soled and silent, nothing to alert the physicist or make him think he was being tailed. By the time he was aware of Kirov's presence, it would be too late to save himself.

Much too late, for both the traitor and his contact.

A car rolled toward them, headlights framing Lenart in silhouette before they swept past. Kirov averted his face from force of habit, idly window-shopping until the vehicle was past and gone.

If they'd been in London, Rome or Paris, news of the shooting at the Rica Victoria would have filled the street with curiosity-seekers jamming the sidewalk in front of the hotel in hopes of seeing anything—a body on a stretcher, uniforms, an ambulance. Norwegians were more private, more restrained. A refreshing change.

And just ahead of them, across the street, was a park, all in darkness now.

Lenart crossed the street, Kirov hanging back in the darkened doorway of a jeweler's shop. The killer watched for traffic, scanning parked cars for indication of surveillance until he was finally satisfied that it wasn't a trap.

He reached beneath his jacket, loosening the silenced pistol in its holster, making ready for a rapid draw if he was taken by surprise. A great, unearthly calm had settled over Kirov as it always did immediately prior to spilling human blood.

And he was smiling as he crossed the street behind Lenart, two shadows merging with the larger darkness of the park.

EMERGING FROM THE HOTEL, Gustave Lenart forgot everything his contact had taught him about shaking surveillance, checking to determine whether he was being followed, watching out for traps. He crossed the hotel lobby like a robot, half-expecting someone's hand to drop upon his shoulder any moment, handcuffs tightening around his wrists.

A midnight stroll.

He'd rehearsed the lie until it echoed in his brain relentlessly. If someone had inquired about the time or told him that his pant legs were on fire, Lenart might well have answered with, "I'm going for a midnight stroll." His nerves were jangling like alarm bells, and he scarcely understood the words of others standing in the lobby as he passed them by, so loudly did his pulse throb in his ears.

Of course, Lenart knew well enough what they were saying. Everyone in the hotel—and half the residents of Lillehammer—were discussing the attack on King Harald. Seven gunmen and five royal security officers had been killed in the attempt, according to the last reports on television. Thirteen members of the conference had been shot, but there was no word yet on the condition of the victims.

Some of them were dead. Lenart knew that from having seen them, having stumbled over bodies and stepped in their blood. All were strangers at a glance as far as he could tell. There had been no sign of Kirov or the handful of other scientists whom he'd recognize. At first that reassurance had cheered him, but he'd caught himself and felt ashamed for gloating at the deaths of others he'd never met.

Outside, he hesitated for the briefest moment in the porte cochere and then turned left in the direction of the park. He knew exactly where to go, but there was time. He didn't have to rush and thereby draw increased attention to himself.

A simple midnight stroll.

He wondered briefly if the gunmen were accounted for, or whether some were still at large. It would be suicide for them to linger on at the hotel, but the idea of snipers lurking in the darkness sent a sharp chill down his spine. It helped a little to remind himself that he wasn't the target of the shooting at the banquet. No one there had given him a second thought.

He found himself excited by the prospect of seeing his contact again, not because she was a lovely woman, but because she represented liberty. With her help he'd soon be free.

How long?

It would be hours yet, of course. They had to reach an airport or a border crossing to depart from Norway, and even a direct flight to the States would take the better part of half a day.

Relax, then. There was time.

The park looked grim, forbidding, on the far side of the street. It was peculiar, Lenart thought, how simple shadows took a place of peace and relaxation and changed it to something dark and sinister. A place to fear.

He hesitated on the curb, hands fisted in his pockets, checking up and down the street. One car had passed him on the walk, and it was heading in the opposite direction. If the driver even saw Lenart, he gave no sign. For once the astrophysicist remembered his instructions, glancing back along the sidewalk, finding no one on his track. He could afford to wait a while and see if anyone appeared, but it seemed foolish, an unhealthy waste of time.

If he was early, he'd wait inside the park where he could hide. The open sidewalk made him feel exposed, a target in a shooting gallery. He could be killed here—by a sniper, or a gunshot from a passing car—and no one might discover him for hours, lying on the pavement while his blood dried rusty brown and he turned cold.

Enough.

He crossed the street with long, determined strides, the very act of movement helping to dispel his fear. The darkness was his friend, a cloak to shelter him from hostile eyes. If anyone was waiting for him in the shadows, it would be his contact.

Monica.

He spoke the name aloud, and found that he was smiling to himself, an almost giddy feeling now that he was safe inside the park. He was a schoolboy cutting class, in search of an adventure, running off to meet a friend—a girl, no less!—and find some better way to pass the time.

Intrigue.

He didn't for a moment think that Monica could ever be attracted to him, interested in him as a man, but this would be his one and only brush with melodrama in an otherwise completely drab and ordinary life. He meant to savor every heartbeat and emotion—fear, exhilaration, come what may. If he was captured, even killed, Lenart would do his best to savor that, as well.

How many men had ever wandered through a foreign city in the dead of night, a gruesome massacre behind them and a lovely woman waiting just ahead? Gustave Lenart, so cloistered until yesterday, felt pity for the millions who would never know their moment in the sun.

Or in the dark.

And this *was* freedom, of a sort. He wanted more, craved everything at once, but if the dream collapsed around him and he got no farther than the park, at least he would have lived. Beyond that, nothing seemed to matter.

The park was fragrant, startling Lenart. Somehow he'd imagined that the trees, shrubs and flowers only shared their perfume in the daylight. Yet another myth destroyed. The schoolboy was learning by experience.

He tried to think, remember, if he had ever walked the streets of Moscow by night. Returning from a lecture or the lab, of course, but it wasn't the same. He knew exactly where to go, his small apartment waiting for him. Empty. Silent. He'd never even kept a pet, as if a small intrusion on the vacuum of his life would somehow emphasize the loneliness and thereby make it real.

Lenart knew he was pitiful, but it no longer mattered now that he had recognized the fact and taken steps to change his life. Whatever happened in the next few moments or the next few years, he'd elected not to sit and wait for time to pass him by. The choice was *his,* and while his enemies could kill him, maybe drag him home in chains, they'd already lost the chance to own his soul.

Gustave Lenart embraced the darkness, moving toward his new life with determination in his stride.

FIVE MINUTES. Close enough. Mack Bolan twisted the ignition key and listened to the car's engine idling smoothly. With the driver's window down he caught a chill breeze off the lake. It smelled of pine trees and exhaust fumes, a peculiar blend of odors spawned by nature dwelling in conjunction with the works of man.

He put the car in motion, rolling gradually toward the park. If he was early, he'd have to make a second pass, and that would spook Lenart. If he was late, the physicist and Monica would fall back to the secondary pickup point and wait five minutes prior to giving up.

It didn't sound like much, but Bolan knew five minutes was a lifetime to a stationary target, waiting for a lift-off that might never come. How many times had he been forced to wait for choppers at a hot LZ in Nam? How many solitary stakeouts had there been, with Bolan shadowing his enemies or staring at them through a sniper scope?

Five minutes was forever.

Forty seconds gone, and Bolan's mind went back to the fiasco at the banquet. There was no ID on any of the shooters yet, but it would come. The Einsatz-gruppe basically used two recruiting pools: the German college campuses and jails. Some of the triggermen were bound to turn up records when the word came back from Interpol, and others might be the subject of a missing person's search at home, with worried parents wondering what had become of little Hans.

Gone to Nazis, every one.

There would have been some word by now if any of the gunmen killed had been the leaders of the Einsatzgruppe. Bolan knew it was too much to hope for, dropping Koch or Norner in a raid like that. The Führer and his right-hand man wouldn't involve themselves in dirty work unless it served some higher purpose.

Or unless the dirty work was absolutely unavoidable.

They had to be running short of troops by now. The news reports had said seven gunmen had died inside the Rica Victoria, pushing the total close to thirty for the week. Assuming every member of the gang had come to Norway, there were roughly ten guns left; perhaps fifteen if he was generous. Enough to cause some trouble if they knew their business, but the group's morale could only be abysmal, with the beatings they'd taken in the past two days. Some might desert the ranks, and he was hoping none of those who stuck would be in perfect fighting trim.

Lenart.

He had to concentrate on business now and get it right the first time.

Bolan had agreed to help Monica with the lift-off, more for something to do than from any personal interest in her charge. Lenart belonged to Langley, but the leak from "Mr. Ragland" to their enemies had ruined any hope Monica had of following the script as written. She couldn't afford to use her contacts now, which meant no pickup driver for the meet, no safehouse, nothing.

Bolan knew it would have been the proper thing for him to check in with Brognola, but he shied away from trusting their last-minute preparations to a transatlantic line. If there had been a chance of help from Stony Man, he might have risked it, but the two of them were on their own.

Three, if you counted the defecting astrophysicist.

A hundred different things could still go wrong, including outside interference from the Company if Monica was being shadowed. Bolan had no special grudge against the CIA; it was like any other agency composed of human beings, some of whom got bent along the way and sold out to the highest bidder. Still, the Executioner had no time for fine distinctions at the moment, and he was in no mood to play games with his enemies.

If anybody tried to stop Lenart from crossing over, they were in for a surprise.

Three minutes.

It was still another quarter mile before he reached the park, and Bolan knew he'd have to dawdle to avoid arriving early. Up ahead a red light helped him out. There was no traffic at the intersection, but the lights kept working either way around the clock.

He thought about Lenart, the kind of culture shock the scientist was going to experience in the United States. For all the knowledge locked inside his brain, Lenart had much to learn. But first they had to get him there.

One minute thirty seconds.

Rolling through the green light, Bolan let his hand drop to the MP-5K submachine gun on the seat beside him. He was ready. If the enemy was waiting, let them do their worst. The Executioner was tired of playing a defensive game.

14

Waiting in the darkness for Lenart, Monica admitted to herself that she was nervous. Things had all been happening so rapidly, with unexpected twists and enemies she hadn't anticipated when she took the job.

From shepherding Lenart she'd been drawn into a very different game, complete with neo-Nazi killers and at least one sellout in the Company itself. Against the odds she'd discovered an amazing ally, but the two of them could only do so much.

She'd considered ways of circumventing her control and touching base with Langley on her own, but it hadn't been feasible within the time she had. From this point on she'd be operating on her own initiative, and there was no way of predicting how her control officer would respond. In theory he could declare her a renegade and cover his own tracks by calling out the guns to silence her forever.

But she still had Mike Belasko on her side, and they'd proved they could work well together—fight together, if it came to that.

She wondered once again about Belasko's people, whether they'd be available for help if things got sticky with Lenart. She hadn't thought it prudent to inquire, but there were many questions preying on her mind as she stood waiting in the dark.

Belasko wasn't with the Company; that much was obvious. She had a working knowledge of the overall intelligence community—the FBI and Secret Service, G-2 and the NSA—but there were doubtless other agencies of which she had no knowledge. Following the murder of her Russian contact, someone in the Company had called for outside help. She didn't understand their motives, but she thanked her lucky stars that it had happened. Otherwise...

She didn't linger on the morbid options. Far from being dead, she was alive and ready to complete her mission. Nothing that her enemies had tried so far had slowed her down. A few more hours, possibly a day, and she'd have Lenart on safer ground. From that point he'd be delivered to a team she could trust...and Monica would have to deal with any consequences of her altered plans.

And she'd have to face the man who had sold her out.

The problems would begin in earnest if she found he wasn't alone. If she'd been set up by Langley, someone higher up the chain of command, then it would be a hopeless case. To vindicate herself she had to start by trusting someone, somewhere. If the Company was riddled with corruption and deceit, then she had nowhere left to turn.

Belasko.

Would he help her—*could* he help her—if it came to breaking with the Company? Could anybody help her?

It occurred to Monica that she might have to help herself. She didn't like the odds, but she hadn't escaped her homeland, entering the service of the CIA, to see her trust abused and twisted into something sinister. The night she'd fled her homeland Monica had been prepared to die. She felt the same determination now, but in a different cause.

Or was it all the same?

She'd been looking for a new life when she slipped away from Prague, a new life free of doubt and fear. Enlisting with the CIA had been a means of paying back the new land that had sheltered her.

But doubt and fear were everywhere. The only way to finally defeat intimidation was to stand your ground and fight. Beginning here and now.

Her ears picked up the sound of footsteps drawing closer. It was still too dark for her to see the new arrival, but he—or she—made no effort to be quiet. Moving closer to the evergreen that sheltered her, Monica slipped a hand inside her bag and came out with the Walther PPK.

How many men would this make if she had to kill again? Four dead and counting.

Lenart was forty feet away before she recognized him.

"Gustave!"

He swiveled toward the sound of her voice, apprehensive at first, breaking out in a cautious smile as she emerged from the shadows. The smile faltered as he saw the pistol in her hand.

"Is anything wrong?"

"Precautions," she replied. "You weren't followed?"

Lenart hesitated, then finally shook his head, and Monica knew he'd forgotten to check. He was excited, frightened. She could hardly blame him in the circumstances. Still ...

"We have to go now."

"Yes, of course."

She was about to stow the automatic in her bag when she heard *other* footsteps, drawing closer. Was it only her imagination?

Lenart frowned and said, "I—"

"Shh!"

No doubt about it now. There was at least one other person with them in the park. She cocked the pistol, slipped her hand back into her shoulder bag and kept it there.

"This way," she whispered. "Quietly."

It seemed as if the footsteps changed direction slightly when they started walking. Monica stopped short, restraining her companion with a hand against his chest. Lenart was clearly frightened now, afraid to speak.

A sudden silence took her by surprise. No footsteps. Nothing. Monica began to count the seconds, reached a minute in her mind, then added fifteen more to allow for a margin of error. This time when they moved she didn't speak, but rather guided Lenart with a hand on his elbow, steering him in the direction of the street. It seemed a hundred miles away, though in reality she knew it was barely fifty yards.

Before they went ten feet a man stepped out in front of them, an automatic pistol in his hand. It was incredible that he could move so silently when moments earlier ...

"Gustave," the stranger said, "I'm disappointed. How could you run off like this without saying good-bye?"

KIROV ENJOYED THE HUNT, letting them hear him at first, then circling around to head them off without a sound. It was a talent, moving silently in darkness. Practice was required, and Kirov kept in practice, prowling through the parks in Moscow. Sometimes he merely watched his prey, but other times . . .

He brought his mind back to the business at hand, smiling at Lenart and his accomplice. A woman. Fairly attractive. Kirov knew her face, but he couldn't immediately place her. It was recent, possibly today, and yet—

Of course!

She had been present at the banquet, serving as a hostess. She hadn't shown Kirov to his seat, but he had noticed her, regardless. In the moment of confusion Kirov almost lost his smile, afraid he hadn't been fully briefed.

No, not afraid. *Concerned.*

He put the problem out of mind and concentrated on the work at hand. The woman was as good as dead no matter who she was or which regime she worked for. Probably American, though he was still confused about her role in the chaotic violence that had marred the banquet. Would his own superiors be interested in knowing which side she was on?

Too late. If they were curious about Lenart's control, they should have briefed him in advance, provided him with pointed questions he could ask her. As it was, Kirov wouldn't know what to stress in an interrogation, and he had no time to spare.

"What are you doing, Vasily?" Lenart's voice sounded coarse and harsh, a product of fear.

"My duty, Gustave. Every patriot must do his duty."

"After all this time?"

The question was supposed to move him, with its implication of a friendship that didn't exist. His smile came back, contemptuous and cold. "I have no sympathy for traitors, Gustave."

If the truth were told, he had no interest in their petty politics at all, but Kirov had a role to play, and he enjoyed the drama of it. Putting on an attitude and making it his own, the same way he had lulled Lenart and all the other lab rats into thinking he was one-dimensional, a cipher like themselves. They looked at his degree and his education and beheld a man with no more depth than the diploma hanging on his wall. It was convenient as a cover, but sometimes it galled him all the same.

"I want to see your hand," he told the woman.

She raised the left one only, showing him the open palm. An infantile delay.

"You had your chance, bitch."

Despite his preparation, even knowing she was armed, the shot still took him by surprise. There was no muzzle-flash, per se—the purse contained it—but he heard the bullet whistle past him, felt it brush his sleeve.

He squeezed a quick shot off in answer, wasting it, intent on seeking cover as the woman fired again. Another miss, and Kirov lost his second silenced round among the trees and shadows. Running, stumbling, it was difficult to aim. Not like the Wild West movies.

Kirov dropped into a fighting crouch and used both hands to brace his weapon as he aimed. The woman had her pistol clear now, aimed in his direction, with her free arm out for balance. Moving past her in the darkness was Lenart.

They fired together, the impact of her .32-caliber projectile rocking Kirov backward on his haunches. Pain and fear exploded through his system as he triggered two quick rounds. Before he landed on his back and rolled away he heard Lenart cry out, a startled sound.

The next shot missed him, and he wriggled backward toward the cover of some evergreens. His side burned where the woman's lucky shot had cracked a rib or two, and blood soaked through his shirt and sport coat.

Damn.

It didn't have the feeling of a mortal wound, but there would still be difficulties. Phone calls. Explanations. Waiting for his masters to provide for a physician he could trust...or finding one himself and silencing the healer afterward. It was a tricky proposition either way. But first he had to stop the woman and Lenart.

Both of them were running now, and Kirov wobbled to his feet. A fresh pain lanced through his side, making him grind his teeth and curse the woman who dared defy him. It was too bad he wouldn't have time to teach her some respect. Her pistol wasn't silenced, and the sounds of gunfire would inevitably draw police. That, coupled with the fact that he was bleeding freely, told the killer he'd have to rush his work.

A simple, no-frills execution. Cut and dried.

He set off in pursuit, first navigating by the sound of footsteps, hesitating when the sound abruptly stopped. They knew he was coming, and the woman hoped to finish him. He hesitated, feeling tremors in his legs, and stood there, listening, his left hand tightly pressed against his wounded side.

They would be moving toward the street. That much was certain. They wouldn't attempt to walk from Lillehammer to an adjacent town, which meant there had to be a vehicle nearby. Perhaps a driver, waiting for the woman's signal. If Kirov waited any longer . . .

Suddenly the footsteps started again, a body crashing through the undergrowth and heading for the street. *One* body? Could it be a trap?

He had no time to waste on speculation. Lurching in pursuit, he felt that he was gaining on his quarry. There would be a clear shot in the final stretch before they reached the curb.

He battered through a clutching hedge and saw Lenart in front of him, an awkward runner glancing back across his shoulder now and then. The woman wasn't visible, and in the heartbeat of decision Kirov knew he'd made a serious mistake.

"Right here."

Her voice behind him was cold and steady as she straightened from her crouch behind the hedge. He looked around, not turning yet, and saw the pistol aimed directly at his face.

What now?

If she was very stupid, she'd try to take him prisoner, disarm him, maybe cuff his hands and leave him there for the authorities. But she didn't look stupid. One glance at her face and Kirov knew he'd have no choice. He had to kill her now before she finished him.

"You win," he told her, desperate for a ploy that would distract her even slightly while he made his move. He was already turning as he spoke, his legs folding under him to throw her aim off and his pistol gliding into target acquisition.

Then there were flashes like a strobe light in his eyes, and something struck his chest with force enough to lift him off his feet, propelling him backward onto the ground. He emptied out the automatic's magazine in rapid fire, but it was wasted on the stars.

How many times had he peered closely at the faces of his victims while they died, the last spark fading, all the time wondering what it must feel like from the other side? Now he knew.

DRIVING WITH HIS WINDOW down, Mack Bolan heard the gunfire from the park and stood on the accelerator, racing toward the sound. He swung in toward the curb and had the MP-5K submachine gun in his hands before the rental car ceased its forward motion. Then he was out the driver's door—the dome light disconnected in advance for safety's sake—and crouched on the lawn prepared for anything, when Monica called out to him.

"Don't shoot! We're coming out."

Two silhouettes emerged from the deeper shadows of the park, and Bolan kept them covered with his stuttergun until he had a visual ID. The woman seemed all right from what he saw. Lenart was limping slightly, and he held his right hand clasped against his left arm just above the elbow.

"In the car. Let's go."

He held the questions back until they boarded and he had the vehicle in motion, rolling north along the avenue. "Is anybody hit?"

"A graze," Monica said, responding for Lenart. "He also sprained his ankle running in the dark."

"That's it?"

"We'll be all right."

"Who jumped you?"

"Kirov." It was the first time Bolan had heard Lenart's voice. "He was supposed to be a friend and colleague."

Bolan glanced at Monica in the shotgun seat and read the expression on her face, knowing he didn't have to ask about the gunman's fate. One down.

"Next stop—"

Before he had a chance to finish the statement a pair of headlights blazed at Bolan from his rearview mirror, moving up behind him like a pair of hungry eyes.

"We've got a tail."

The warrior had no way of telling who it was behind them, and he didn't particularly care. They had to shake off their pursuers quickly now in case the trackers were in contact with a plug team up ahead. There was no time to waste.

The dark sedan swung out to pass them on the left, accelerating in a move to overtake and pass. A muzzle-flash erupted from the right-rear window, and he heard the impact of a bullet on the car's fender. Monica had swiveled in her seat and cranked her window down, the Walther blazing back at their pursuers.

"Try this."

He handed her the MP-5K submachine gun, holding steady on the wheel to let her aim. There were more muzzle-flashes from the tail car as it hung in close pursuit, a miss immediately followed by the loud thump of a ricochet across the trunk.

Beside him Monica was leaning out the window, sighting with the stuttergun and squeezing off a measured burst. He lost the tail car for a moment, then saw it swerve, but the driver tried to save himself too late. The windshield seemed to fog and then imploded in a storm of fractured safety glass. There was another burst in parting, then their adversaries jumped the curb and plowed head-on into a darkened storefront.

Bolan took the next street on their right and left the avenue to find another route, alert to any sign of fresh pursuit. Behind them there was only darkness, and the same lay up ahead. He glanced across at Monica and handed her a fresh clip for the H&K.

"They had us spotted going in," he said.

"It would appear so."

Bolan's frown was angry in the muted dashboard lights. "We need to give this plan some second thought."

"Such as?"

"A little twist to throw them off the track."

15

The new plan called for a complete revision of their course. Plan A had called for a direct run south to Oslo, where arrangements could be made for a departure via air or sea. It was a variation of the plan devised by Monica's control, but he'd hoped to pull it off regardless. Sheer audacity could sometimes make the difference in a pinch, but Bolan recognized that they'd lost their edge in Lillehammer well before they hit the road.

The setup in the park was one thing. Theoretically, anyone could have tailed Lenart from the hotel and tried to take him out before he made the jump. A motorized pursuit was something else entirely. It suggested planning in advance, or else a more sophisticated surveillance than they'd anticipated. In the worst scenario it meant they were burned from start to finish, whether by Monica's link to the Company or some other source. The only thing they could do to salvage something from the wreckage was to scrub Plan A and chart a new approach.

Which brought them to Plan B.

The run due west would take them through the heart of Norway's central mountains to the fjord country on the coast. From there, with any luck, they could arrange for transport to England or the continent. But first they had to get there.

It was a journey of almost four hundred miles, but they'd be confined to winding mountain roads for much of that, with ferry crossings indicated on the last leg of their run. A fair head start should let them hold a decent lead, but they would be in trouble if their adversaries got ahead of them and set up an ambush.

The ferry crossing Lake Mjosa was their first hurdle, and Monica had bandaged Lenart's bullet graze by the time they drove on board. They used the time in transit to chart their course, Bolan memorizing checkpoints on the way. Their first stop would be Gausdal, rolling on from there to Fagernes, and then due north. They could make better time by keeping to the main highway west of Fagernes, but that would be the route their enemies would expect if they tried to plot an ideal western course. They'd head northwest into Nordberg, Grotil and Geiranger, boarding the Geiranger ferry for a last run out to Alesund on the coast.

And if they couldn't find a boat or seaplane outward bound from there, they'd be trapped.

At least cash wouldn't be a problem. Bolan's luggage held plenty. In addition to the money, they had two handguns plus the MP-5K submachine gun, extra magazines for each and half a dozen hand grenades. Unless they met an army on the road, it ought to see them through...but Bolan was experienced enough to hold off on predicting the future.

There were still too many unknown variables in the game for Bolan to relax and let himself feel comfortable. The trap in Lillehammer had been neatly baited, and he couldn't shake the feeling that Monica's control was playing games.

"You haven't been in touch with anyone at all since yesterday?" he asked again.

She shook her head emphatically. "They knew about the park, of course, but they had no idea about the day or time."

"It could have been a standing watch," Bolan said, but the explanation had a hollow ring.

"I should have taken time to see if Kirov had a radio."

"There wasn't any time to spare," he said. "You did all right."

"I don't like having people watch me all the time. It makes me feel like some kind of specimen."

"You might consider changing jobs."

"I might at that."

"We'd better finish this one first."

"Agreed."

Lenart said little on the first leg of their trip, retreating into anxious silence as he watched the miles roll by. A time or two Bolan had felt the scientist watching him and glanced up in time to meet Lenart's gaze in the rearview mirror. He would have liked to smile, perhaps say something reassuring, but it didn't seem to fit the circumstances. It was better for Lenart to stay alert, a bit on edge, than to deceive himself by thinking they were home and dry.

The game could still go either way, but it wasn't in Bolan's nature to go down without a fight.

At least he had one ally he could count on. Monica had proved herself on three occasions now, and he'd trust her with his life if it came down to that. Meanwhile the Executioner would do his very best to reach the coast without confrontation on the way.

The radio gave out a nonstop stream of news about the failed assassination effort, mentioning the Einsatzgruppe specifically as they were rolling into Gausdal. There was still no mention of the neo-Nazi leadership, their whereabouts or any prospect for arrests.

No news was bad news this time out. It meant a number of their enemies were still at large, and while the neo-Nazis should logically be scrambling for cover, running for their lives, they'd already demonstrated a disturbing propensity for turning up at the wrong place and time.

He stopped for gas in Gausdal, knowing that Norwegian filling stations were few and far between, preferring a delay of his own choosing to the risk of running low on fuel when there was no more to be had.

They were racing the clock now, as well as their enemies. And Bolan was uncomfortably aware that no one ever really beat the march of time.

THE PHONE RANG TWICE, three times, before a weary voice responded on the other end. Alexandrei Rostov took a near-sadistic pleasure in the sound of Eric Norner's tone.

"Your soldiers missed again, I see."

He could imagine Norner bristling, knuckles blanching as he clenched the telephone receiver.

"We were told that her support had been withdrawn," the neo-Nazi snapped. "Instead, we find a driver waiting, armed with automatic weapons. I can't be held responsible for failed intelligence."

Touché. Rostov resisted the impulse to curse Norner's family lineage going back six generations, putting on the next best thing to a conciliatory tone.

"It seems the lady might have gone in business for herself. She has been out of touch with her superiors since yesterday, the business at the restaurant."

"And you expect my men to find her now? Impossible!"

"Not quite. Provisions have been made. A fallback option, as our friends in the United States would say."

"I'm listening." There was suspicion in the German's voice, as if he feared he was being led astray deliberately. Too bad, for Norner's sake, that he wasn't a bit more paranoid. If so, he might save himself.

"Suffice to say we have a means of following her progress, courtesy of those she left behind."

"You've found her, then?"

"We never lost her, Eric. You need faith."

"I need more men!" the neo-Nazi countered bitterly.

"Recruitment is beyond my province, I'm afraid. Of course, you'll need more cash for an enlistment drive when this job's been completed to our mutual satisfaction."

"I'll do everything I can," Norner said, knowing he was trapped.

"This time I thought it might be helpful if you undertook the chore yourself."

There was another hesitation on the far end of the line, and Rostov pictured Norner scowling, possibly consulting with his bosom buddy Dieter Koch.

"I normally avoid such personal entanglements," the neo-Nazi said at last.

"I wouldn't call these normal circumstances, Eric. Would you? A failure now on top of everything and I'm very much afraid my backers would insist on finding a more worthwhile charity for their support."

"I understand."

Regardless of the native language, the Americans were right on one score. Money talked.

"You'll have to hurry, I'm afraid," Rostov said. "It appears your rabbit is attempting to establish a substantial lead."

"I'll need an hour more or less."

"No more." The steel was back in Rostov's tone as he began to dictate highways and coordinates, repeating when he had to, making sure Norner got it all.

"It shall be done," the German promised after Rostov finished with his travelog.

"I hope so, Eric. I've enjoyed our partnership so far. I would be gravely disappointed if it had to end unhappily."

"Have faith."

"I do."

He cradled the receiver, then glanced up at Thadden and Svoboda in their armchairs, each man watching him with rapt attention.

"So?" the stodgy German asked at last.

"The Einsatzgruppe is in pursuit," Rostov stated, putting on a smile he didn't feel.

"Perhaps they'll get it right this time," Svoboda said contemptuously.

"And if not," Rostov said, "we shall be there to assist them."

There was instant silence in the room as his comrades stared at him over their brandy snifters.

"How?" Svoboda blurted out. "I mean..."

"The same way Norner's people will keep track of their intended prey." He paused just long enough to take advantage of the silence, letting tension build. "The woman's handbag."

"Eh?" Svoboda was a little slow that evening, what with all the news his brain had been ordered to absorb since nine o'clock.

"A micro-homer," Rostov explained. "Installed by the Americans without her knowledge. On the one hand, it allows her contact to be warned if she encounters any risk or deviates from her routine. In this case, all he has to do is pass the information on."

"I'm still confused," Thadden said. "If they want the woman dead, why don't the bastards simply kill her on their own?"

"The woman is of no significance," Rostov said, feeling like the tutor of a very backward child. "Some of the Americans are wise enough to share our mutual concern about the recent change of course in Eastern Europe. We're losing territory, but the CIA is simultaneously losing enemies. You understand? Some people in the Company prefer the devils they know to a new crop of unfamiliar demons."

"Or," Thadden suggested with a chuckle, "unemployment if they find no devils to oppose."

"The possibility has been discussed, I can assure you."

Thadden raised his snifter, offering a toast. "The *true* détente," he jeered.

"But how can we assist the Einsatzgruppe?" Svoboda asked, still chewing on the problem Rostov had raised.

"Strategic backup if they need it," the Russian said. "More important, we can assure they don't survive to boast about their work. Our press releases on the martyrdom of German manhood will be more than adequate to state the fascist case."

"They might be useful in the future," Thadden said.

"With this behind them? So much bad publicity?" The Russian shook his head. "They wouldn't last a month at large in Europe, anywhere on earth. If we need other neo-Nazis in the future, we can always raise them up as we did these. There seems to be no shortage in the field of candidates."

Appreciative laughter made a circuit of the room, then died away. They knew it was time to move, but no one was jumping at the chance to put the thought into words.

"Pack lightly," Rostov ordered at last, asserting his authority. "Ten minutes at the car downstairs."

They left him, muttering to each other but he knew they'd obey. They had no choice if they intended to keep on receiving stipends from the KGB to work their dirty schemes around Berlin and Prague. Without his backing they'd lapse into obscurity and fade away to nothing, an intolerable fate for men who had a taste of power and had found it addictive.

Rostov spent the next five minutes checking out his Steyr AUG and extra magazines, breaking the futuristic assault rifle down for a tidier fit in his suitcase before he checked out of his room. The others would be more or less on time, but he intended to be waiting at the car before them. One more object lesson in commitment to the cause before they hit the road.

And if they didn't all return intact . . . well, that was life, survival of the fittest in a world where it was dog-eat-dog. Tonight, Rostov thought, he would be the leanest, meanest dog of all. He would be positively rabid as they closed in for the kill.

NORNER AND KOCH rode together in the lead car, a Mercedes, with Gunther Pries behind the wheel. Juergen Bartsch made four. The second vehicle, a Volkswagen, was driven by Karl Hochler, with Werner Heydrich in command. The back-seat gunners would be Horst Jaegerhof and Heini Kurten.

Eight men, all armed, and Dieter Koch still wondered what would happen if they failed. Unfortunately his imagination offered him no shortage of dramatic options, all of them eventually climaxed by a death scene he'd rather not play out.

They barely made the Lake Mjosa ferry on its last run of the night. The dark water was speckled with reflected stars, and it was frosty-cold where Koch stood at the railing, drawing on a cigarette.

"I don't like any of this, Eric."

"No."

They'd agreed on that much from the last call, anyway, but neither one could find a ready way to sever the connection with their demanding sponsors. There was more to saying no than simply losing out on future contracts and repaying money fronted in advance. A bailout in the middle of it meant they were unreliable, and unreliable assassins might be tempted to unload their information on police if they were ever run to ground and squeezed.

Rejecting this phase of the operation would have been the next best thing to suicide. Their sponsors would have had no choice but to silence them forever as a means of self-defense.

Case closed.

Koch wondered to himself sometimes exactly how much he'd sacrifice to see the triumph of the master race. In theory it was all or nothing, but a man still had priorities. If called upon to suffer mutilation, for example, could he pick the body parts at random and not miss them after they were gone? How would he bear up under torture if the information wanted by his enemies seemed relatively trivial? If he were called upon to die . . .

Stop that!

Sometimes Koch honestly believed their disciples in the ranks were better off with only half a brain per man. They learned to hate, picked up the basic Nazi jargon soon enough and waded in when there was dirty work to do. When they were off the clock, a stein of beer and something warm to wrap their arms around was all a trooper asked for. Few if any of them contemplated grand designs, the Day of Victory or what would lie beyond.

The Day of Victory.

Some days Koch had to ask himself if it was more than just a pipe dream that he shared with Eric Norner. When Hitler rallied millions to his fighting banner, it had been a simpler time, with people anxious for an opportunity to pin their economic woes on greedy Jews. Today, despite the victory of national reunion and a rising martial spirit in the land, it was more difficult to garner wide support for radical beliefs. The people of the Reich had grown complacent over time, seduced by fairy tales about the Holocaust that painted Himmler and his SS heroes in the role of rabid beasts.

The Einsatzgruppe had started out originally as an educational society to help the people learn their history, restore their racial pride. The other business, all that had followed, was an afterthought of sorts . . . or had it always been foremost on Norner's mind?

It was too late for Koch to second-guess the movement now. For good or ill his lot was cast, and he could no more change the recent past than he could change his bloodline. Aryans were bound by fate to stand and fight together, die together if they failed in their attempt to save the Western world. Extinction of the master race was preferable to its subjugation under mongrel species that would fasten leechlike on the body of the people and drain off their vitality.

Koch felt his anger mounting, as it always did when he let his mind dwell on the perfidy of his opponents. Worst of all were those enfeebled onetime Aryans who helped the Jews and other mongrels to corrupt the planet for their private gain. The Einsatzgruppe would have ways to deal with them when it was time.

The thought stopped Koch cold when he remembered that at the moment there were barely twelve men living in the Einsatzgruppe, and eight of those were sandwiched into cars, borne off in hot pursuit of enemies they couldn't even name. The woman who had murdered several of their men, and who—in Koch's mind, anyway—was probably a Jew planted by the Mossad. And a so-called scientist defecting from his homeland, who was almost certainly an egghead Jewish "thinker," fit for nothing but the routine of the laboratory.

And a third man, still unknown, the driver, who could also fight, as witnessed by the raids on Thursday afternoon and evening.

That one was a warrior, never mind his race or politics. It would be difficult to track him, harder still to corner him and take him down. With all that he'd seen in the past two days, Koch wondered if an eight-man team was equal to the task.

No matter. It was all they had, and it would have to do.

The mental loop had come full circle, and he did his best to shut it off. Reflections on mortality weren't his strong suit. When Koch was theorizing, he preferred to set his mind on victory, the triumph of a world where Aryans reigned supreme and the subject races knew their place. In time, when reproduction quotas were achieved by pure-blood newlyweds, the slave class would become expendable.

The final solution finally achieved.

It was a great day to anticipate, and Koch's vision kept him smiling as they ferried over Lake Mjosa, smiling still as they unloaded in the darkness on the other side.

Whatever lay ahead his sacrifice was nothing in comparison to the intended goal. A world of perfect men and women, raising families in perfect harmony. And if they had to spill some blood meanwhile to realize that dream, then who was Koch to complain?

16

Otto Thadden drove the first leg of their journey, Rostov navigating, while Svoboda sat in back beside the duffel bag that held their weapons, speaking only when he was addressed directly. With the map spread on his knees, a penlight in his hand, Rostov was trying to anticipate the movements of his enemies.

One beauty of the landscape spread in front of them was its simplicity. The mountains helped him here by making road construction difficult and costly. Unlike France and Spain, much less America, there weren't ten or fifteen different routes they could use to reach a given town. Once Rostov's prey turned north from Fagernes, they had one track and only one to Randsverk, about 120 miles away. From this point on it all came down to speed.

He reckoned the Einsatzgruppe commandos would be somewhere ahead of them, but he could only guess how far. Ideally they'd overtake the fugitives and finish it before Rostov and his reluctant companions had to become more directly involved. If not . . .

He was prepared for anything by this time, less concerned about Lenart as a defector than the fact that his connection with the CIA had broken ranks and was apparently proceeding on her own initiative without controls. The break with her superiors, taken in conjunction with the bungled ambush at the Holmenkollen restaurant, could only mean she had made her contact—"Mr. Ragland"—as a turncoat. She could link him to the Einsatzgruppe operation with her own eyewitness testimony, and Rostov had no doubt that "Ragland" would prefer to spill his guts in lieu of spending twenty years to life in Leavenworth. Once he began to talk, there would be no end to embarrassment for all concerned.

Another reason why they had to stop the runners cold before they found a way to leave the country was that it was so much easier than taking out a chief of station for the CIA. Less fuss, less muss. And if he found a way to spare his contact with the Company, it meant that Rostov could continue dealing with the CIA at will, albeit once removed.

A link like that was worth its weight in gold and couldn't be discarded casually, but if it had to go...

He wished there was some way he could get in touch with Norner now that they were on the road. A simple progress check from time to time would make things easier, but there had been no way to do it short of setting up a link that could rebound against him and betray him if the game went wrong.

No need, he told himself. If Norner's people found Lenart and company, there would be evidence along the highway, maybe littering the streets of some small town. Police would be involved, and there would be no way to keep the confrontation secret. If they didn't see the wreckage for themselves, reports would certainly be broadcast on the radio.

A part of Rostov almost hoped Norner and his Einsatzgruppe bullies missed their prey. It would be good to join the hunt again firsthand instead of sitting in an office and directing others, playing an elaborate game within the KGB, but there were times when he missed joining in on the dirty work himself, invading homes and embassies, pursuing traitors on a narrow country lane at midnight, staring into frightened eyes as he squeezed off a killing shot.

The good times.

If it came down to killing, he could count on Thadden to support him. What the German lacked in brilliance and imagination he made up in ruthless courage, ever ready to confront an enemy and grind him into pulp. Svoboda was a different kind of animal, despite his former role as an interrogator with the STB. He didn't mind inflicting pain on helpless captives, but he didn't feel at ease in situations where his human prey was armed and capable of striking back.

It took all kinds, Rostov thought, and the Party was sometimes compelled to work with sorry specimens. The emphasis was on obedience, and those who followed orders were rewarded for their contributions to the cause.

They might not be the best men for the job, all things considered, but they were the only troops available to Rostov at the moment. They would have to do.

And if they failed him, then Rostov would simply have to do the job himself.

IN OTHER CIRCUMSTANCES Monica would have preferred to make the drive by daylight. They were winding through majestic mountains the Norwegians christened Jotunheimen—"home of the giants"—and she knew the scenery was spectacular, with snow-capped peaks, stark cliffs, white-water rapids, plunging waterfalls. It was a tourist paradise where every scenic turnout offered panoramic views of stunning beauty.

Even so tonight the darkness was their only friend.

Once they had started north from Fagernes, with no diversions possible until they entered Randsverk and turned west toward Lom, she spent a fair amount of time examining the road behind them, half-turned in her seat, working with the mirror mounted on her door. The mountain roads were such that no pursuer would attempt to run without his lights—or live long if he did—but frequent curves and switchbacks also minimized their view of cars approaching from behind. Still, there were moments when the road curved back upon itself and she could see for miles—or could have in the daylight—and she watched incessantly for headlights on their track.

And saw them five miles out of Beitostolen, running well behind.

Her companion checked his rearview mirror, slowing at the next full curve until the lights came into view. At first it seemed to be one car, but then a second came into view. Four headlights shone in the darkness like two pair of rodent eyes.

He didn't speak, but he began to drive a little faster after that, braking less on the curves, relying on a shift of gears. Monica felt his urgency and kept her fingers crossed, still hoping it might be an innocent coincidence. Norwegians used their roads at any hour of the day or night, like anybody else. There was no reason why the lights behind them had to indicate an enemy, and every reason why she should assume they weren't.

How could the hunters track them now that they'd ditched the Oslo run in favor of another plan unknown to Monica's control? If they had troops enough to cover every road and highway leading out of Lillehammer, inspecting every town along the way, then it was hopeless. But she didn't think that was the case.

The Einsatzgruppe had suffered massive casualties, perhaps two-thirds of its recorded strength, and they should have no motive for pursuing her in any case. Unless...

She thought about her contact, "Ragland," trying to decide what kind of bargain he'd struck. Protection for himself, of course. The kind of insulation that would leave him looking squeaky clean if anything went wrong. He wouldn't touch the neo-Nazis with a ten-foot pole, but if the Einsatzgruppe was available to serve the common interest of a small cartel, then buffers could be used. In theory "Ragland" wouldn't even have to know about the move against King Harald. It would be enough for him to understand that something had been planned to scuttle *perestroika* in the West and help return the cold war to status quo.

It was incredible, the more she thought about it, that a man or group of men concerned about their jobs could push the continent—indeed, the world—toward war. It didn't startle her that men would do such things—she had enough experience with human avarice by now to understand that anything was thinkable—but it dismayed her that they had the means, the power, to achieve their goal.

What could she ever hope to do against such men?

Destroy them, given half a chance.

It was a calculated gamble, but she still believed there must be men of loyalty and principle at Langley, heading the Company. If all of them were implicated in the Ragland plan, then she was doomed. But it would only take one friendly ear, one finger on the panic button, to disrupt the plan and bring it crashing down.

She glanced back at Lenart and found him huddled in a corner, staring back along the winding mountain road. His brush with death in Lillehammer had left him frightened. The thought of being overtaken by their enemies had him trembling where he sat. Her heart went out to him, remembering her own defection to the West.

Their track wound ever upward, dipping here and there but always climbing once again to where the peaks were wreathed in clouds. Belasko's vision was restricted here, and they were forced to creep along instead of fleeing full speed from their enemies. The only consolation, if it could be called that, was the thought that anyone behind them would be hampered by the same conditions. On the other hand, if they should stop and lay an ambush while they had a chance...

She put the thought away, imagining a carload of innocent tourists looming out of the mist, swerving toward the sheer cliff under fire. If it went over, they'd never know who they'd killed, or whether the attack had been in vain.

Drive on then. Try to hold a lead and pray for open ground on which to make their stand if they couldn't escape. Two cars mean they'd surely be outnumbered, but Belasko was an expert, and Monica had discovered in herself a surprising facility for combat.

It disturbed her, in a way, the ease with which she'd adapted to a violent life-style. Even after Langley's training, all the martial arts and weapons courses, she'd never really planned on killing anyone. And yet within the past week she'd killed at least five men—perhaps more, with the chase car she'd riddled back in Lillehammer. Part of what disturbed her was the fact that she didn't feel worse, more traumatized at having taken human life.

She told herself that it was self-defense, a part of carrying out her assignment, but she understood there was more involved. Instead of feeling plain relief when she escaped a killing situation, Monica experienced the satisfaction of a job well done. Not the elation of a hunter's kill, but something more like what she thought a soldier must experience when he survived a close encounter on the battlefield.

And she could understand why certain fighting men extended tours of duty, hiring on as mercenaries if their homelands had no wars available. It could become addictive, this excitement balanced on the razor's edge of fear.

She took a breath and held it, concentrating on the road behind them. On the darkness.

Watching for their enemies.

"UP THERE!"

Koch pointed over Norner's shoulder toward the looming darkness of the mountain peak. His eyes had picked out something like a firefly, there and gone but coming back again—a smudge of headlights far above them, following the spiral road.

"It could be someone else," Norner said, straining forward with his hand braced on the dash.

"At this hour?"

"Early risers. How the hell should I know?"

"I can smell them," Koch told him, watching as the headlights showed themselves again.

The trick was catching up on such a road, with endless twists and turns, where they were seldom able to escape from second gear. The straightaways were few and far between, so steep he could feel the engine straining as they climbed. One slip, an oversight produced by haste, and they'd plummet to a fiery death.

Koch wondered if his heart would stop from fright before he hit the bottom and the car disintegrated. He could almost picture it—the headlong plunge with everyone around him screaming, clutching at their seats as if a firm grip on the car would mitigate a drop of several hundred feet. Would there be something close to pleasure in the final seconds of the drop?

It would be better, he decided, to stand back and watch his enemies go over. Better still to shoot them first, disable them but leave them breathing as he pushed their car across the brink. There would be a final scraping sound before they toppled into empty space, his laughter blotting out their desperate cries.

It was a handsome fantasy, but he couldn't count on his adversaries to cooperate. So far they'd been ruthless and resourceful, striking boldly in defiance of the Einsatzgruppe's guns. It troubled Koch that they didn't even have a head count on their enemies. A woman and a man, besides the Czech defector... but suppose they had acquired more reinforcements in the meantime?

Never mind.

The wheel was turning, and he felt a need to take revenge upon his enemies. There was a price to pay for making sport of heroes, and the bill was overdue. He would enjoy humiliating those who tried to sabotage the movement in its infancy.

He rummaged in the duffel bag that held their weapons, smuggled in by Norner's contact. In the bag were two Skorpions, an AK-47 and a Franchi automatic shotgun packing riot loads. If they could simply overtake their prey, it should be relatively simple, blasting at the car nonstop until they drove it off the road.

It was almost an anticlimax when he thought about it that way. It was only fitting they should suffer for the problems they had caused, but he couldn't manipulate the circumstances of the chase to suit himself. It was enough to know that they died screaming, conscious of their grievous error at the last.

Koch glanced behind him, satisfied to see that Heydrich's car was keeping pace. If he could see their prey ahead, however faintly, then their own lights must be visible to those whom they pursued.

So be it. Let the filthy race traitors tremble as they ran, aware that death was breathing down their necks. If they got careless, took a curve too swiftly in the dark, so much the better. Koch could watch them die and never waste a round of ammunition in the process.

"Are you sure it's them?" The question came from Gunther Pries behind the wheel, hunched forward like a man who thought his posture could propel a car at greater speed.

Beside him Norner held the monitor his contact had supplied, no larger than a pack of cigarettes. It filled their automobile with a steady hum. "Who else?"

"Just asking." Pries sounded out of sorts. "I mean . . . what's this? They're gone!"

Above them Koch could see no trace of headlights now, but he was certain the road should still be visible. It wouldn't crest the mountain and begin its downward winding path for close to half a mile.

"The clouds," Koch said at last with total confidence. "They've driven into clouds. It ought to slow them down."

"And us," the driver grumbled, talking to himself.

"Come on, then, while you have a chance. More speed!"

Koch reached back into the bag and lifted out a Skorpion. It felt good in his hands, a comforting weight. He could depend upon the weapon, where another man might fail him in emergencies. He knew his own skill with a firearm, and he trusted the machine to do its job.

Soon now.

17

Near dawn they stopped at a Lapp trading post to change drivers, with Monica taking the wheel. The outpost was a combination mobile home and lean-to, with smoke curling lazily from a chimney in back. Out front the items on perpetual display included antlers, hides and hand-carved wooden trolls. A pair of drowsy reindeer raised their heads to check the new arrivals out, but they weren't alarmed by what they saw.

Lenart stayed where he was, preferring to remain inside the car, although they offered him a chance to stretch his legs. They had apparently picked up some time on their pursuers in the clouds and mist, but Bolan knew it would be premature to let himself relax. If those were gunmen on their track—and he had little doubt of that—it would take more than winding curves and spotty fog to throw them off the scent.

One problem that repeated in his mind was method. How could their pursuers—neo Nazi, Red or otherwise—have narrowed down the search so rapidly? There were different routes they could have taken, all within an hour's drive of Lillehammer, and Bolan still didn't believe their opposition had the numbers for a blanket sweep of central Norway. The alternative could only be a leak, but once again the question came back: how?

"The luggage," Bolan said as Monica was turning the ignition key.

"Excuse me?"

"They needed some kind of an edge to track us down. There has to be a homer somewhere in the car."

"We don't have time—"

"I'm gambling now," he said. "The only luggage I'm sure of is the set I brought with me. We have to ditch the rest right now."

She didn't hesitate. "All right."

They emptied the bag of weapons, ditching it along with the suitcase Monica had stowed in the trunk preparatory to their departure. If the Lapps could find some use for the discarded personal effects, so much the better.

"And your handbag," Bolan added. "Keep your wallet, passport, anything you need for traveling, but lose the bag."

Again no protest, though he caught a glance from Monica that said she thought he might be going overboard. A moment later they were on the road again.

"Suppose it's in the car?" she asked when they had traveled half a mile.

"Then we just wasted time we can't afford," he answered, checking out the right-hand mirror as he spoke.

Still nothing on their tail, but logic told him they were running out of time. Unless he'd been wrong about the trackers—or unless a miracle occurred and both chase cars broke down along the way—they could expect to see the pursuit vehicles before much longer.

Daybreak in the mountains was an awe-inspiring sight. The rising sun lent pastel colors to the clouds and jagged peaks around them, slowly burning off a major portion of the haze. In any other circumstances Bolan would have said it had the makings of a lovely day.

But there were no good days for being hunted like an animal. The daylight only made it that much easier for trackers to pursue their prey, and all the running fox could hope for was the chance to see another sundown when the darkness would conceal his spoor.

Unless he turned upon the hunters and gave them something to remember for their trouble.

The logistics held him back. He trusted Monica to pull her weight and more in any confrontation with the enemy, but there was still Lenart to think of, and their stock of ammunition was depleted following their clashes with the Einsatzgruppe. An ill-considered effort to reverse the game would spell disaster if his timing or evaluation of the odds were off by so much as a fraction.

Better to continue running for the moment, Bolan thought, than to discard his momentary lead in favor of a move that might prove suicidal.

"Look!"

He followed Monica's direction, glancing back at the road behind them just in time to see a dark sedan appear. Behind it, trailing by a length of twenty yards or so, a second car rolled into view.

The hunters, right.

"Hang on!" Monica snapped.

"WE HAVE THEM!" Norner blurted, hunching forward in his seat, an automatic pistol in his hand. "Speed up!"

"I have the road to think of," the driver told him through clenched teeth.

"Forget the road! Hurry! Run them down!"

He switched hands with the pistol, cranking down his window. Mountain air as cold and sharp as razors swept Norner's hair back, stinging his eyes. No matter. He could still see well enough to make a killing shot at point-blank range.

A glance behind confirmed the chase car hanging on their bumper, weapons visible as Heydrich and his people braced themselves for contact. Any moment now...

They had continued through the night, not even taking time to rotate drivers once they had finally emerged from the encroaching clouds. It was impossible to say if their intended prey had spotted them before the shrouding mist had closed in, but they couldn't take any chances with the enemy in sight.

And then, among the clouds, the enemy was *not* in sight for nearly two hours, vanished, while they had labored along in the reflected glare of their own headlights, fighting to keep up. The winding curves were treacherous, with Gunther Pries shifting down and craning forward in his seat to scan the road. When they broke through at last near dawn, it had seemed that their prey had given them the slip.

It all had come down to speed then, Norner perfectly aware that they had missed no turnoffs on the way. If nothing else, the homing monitor had confirmed that Lenart and his companions were ahead of them somewhere.

Until they had passed the sleepy trading post a short while after dawn. The signal from the monitor was suddenly *behind* them, forcing Pries to apply the brakes and back uphill around the curve, no room for turning on the narrow mountain track.

They'd found the small pile of discarded luggage, and Norner had cursed bitterly as he'd demanded speed. The sun would be their ally now, and there was nowhere for his enemies to run except downhill.

And now he had them back.

"Move in!"

"I'm *moving* in! We don't have wings, you know."

Behind him Koch and Juergen Bartsch had rolled their windows down, and wind was whipping through the car, a minihurricane that swept coherent speech away, forcing Norner to shout if he wanted his instructions heard.

He thrust his head and shoulder out the window, cold eyes narrowed into slits against the rushing wind, tears blowing back into his hairline as he braced his elbow on the door and tried to aim his automatic. Norner's first shot was a throwaway, completely wasted, but it helped him to correct his aim.

The second shot was closer, chipping flakes of paint from the left rear fender, near the speeding auto's taillight. Poor, but it was still a hit, and he corrected for the third round, shifting up and to the right. If he could wound the driver, even startle him enough to send him spinning off the road . . .

Koch chose that moment to unleash a wild burst from his Skorpion, the bullets rustling past Norner's head with a sound that made him flinch, his third shot going wild.

"Goddamn!"

Even Bartsch was firing now, and Norner ducked his head back into the car to keep from getting picked off by his own men. It mattered little in the long run whose shot brought the runners down as long as they were stopped without delay.

"Move up! Get closer!"

Pries muttered something underneath his breath, but it was lost in the confusion and he did as he was told. The downhill slope provided greater impetus for their acceleration. He could almost drop the gearshift into neutral and let gravity take over, turning the Mercedes into a guided projectile of death.

Too much, Norner thought as his free hand clutched the dashboard. He had no desire to make himself a martyr in the cause—not yet, at any rate. He meant to stand above the corpses of his enemies—symbolically, if nothing else—and gloat at their destruction after all the havoc they had wrought.

Soon now.

Another moment, two at most.

"Get *up* there, dammit! Ram them if you have to!"

Pries cursed and stood on the accelerator, wrenching at the wheel as they approached another hairpin turn. "Hang on, for Christ's sake!"

"Do it!"

Norner braced himself and held the pistol in his lap, prepared to fire the instant he was presented with a target. And the next time, Norner vowed, he wouldn't miss.

ALEXANDREI ROSTOV brought his car around the mountain crest and glimpsed another car several curves below him, hurrying along. In front of that were two more, engaged in what appeared to be a close pursuit.

"We have them," he informed the others, smiling for the first time since he'd found the woman's luggage with the homer dumped beside the highway some miles back.

"Those must be Norner's people," Thadden guessed. "They made good time."

"They might yet do our work," Rostov said, hoping it was true. "We have to wait and see."

"They have enough guns surely," Svoboda said, craning forward from his place in back.

"They had enough guns *every* time," Rostov replied without emotion. "They need nerves and skill as well as hardware."

"I'd say the driver in that chase car has some nerve," Thadden commented, watching as the first two cars raced out of sight around another bend.

"He smells a kill," Rostov said, familiar with the feeling from his own experience. It was intoxicating, having come so far and risked so much, when suddenly the quarry was within your grasp. The urge to risk it all, dare anything in the pursuit of victory, was overwhelming—nearly irresistible.

And it was at such moments, Rostov knew, when an enlightened hunter had to guard against his own enthusiasm, hanging back to watch and wait a bit, alert to any hidden traps. It was so easy in the heat of battle to betray yourself and lose it all.

But not this time.

He had the Einsatzgruppe serving as his point men, closing on the targets even now, and he was close enough to throw his own weight in at any moment if the battle seemed to go against his side.

And if the neo-Nazis were successful, he'd still be close enough to finalize the plan, insert the final pieces in the puzzle, watch it all fall into place.

The Einsatzgruppe had outlived its usefulness, or nearly so. A few more moments, either way, and Rostov could dispense with Norner's baby Hitlers. When their work was done, they'd continue serving Rostov in a new capacity.

As scapegoats.

Dead scapegoats.

There would be nothing in the way of leaks or startling revelations at the trial, since there would *be* no trial. Dead men could hardly answer their accusers in the press, and once the Nazi link to Lillehammer's bloodbath was confirmed, the media rumor mill would roll along quite nicely on its own. Before you knew it—

"Shooting now."

He couldn't hear the gunshots with the windows closed, the engine sounds and rush of wind around them, but they followed Thadden's pointing finger toward the lead cars—visible again for just a moment—and he saw the Einsatzgruppe gunmen firing. Chips of paint flew off the lead car's trunk before it whipped around another curve, the gunners in pursuit.

They couldn't last much longer, hopelessly outnumbered, racing down a winding dead-end track with nothing but the Geiranger Fjord ahead of them. It was a box with only one way out, and Rostov was prepared to slam the door if anyone slipped past the neo-Nazis at the final moment.

"Be ready," he commanded, feeling Thadden reach down for the heavy bag between his feet. Svoboda muttered something unintelligible, but when Rostov glimpsed his image in the rearview mirror, the little Czech had a Skorpion machine pistol in his hands.

"Whatever happens now," he told his two companions, "there could still be loose ends that need cleaning up."

"STAY DOWN!"

Lenart was on the floor already, huddled in between the seats, but he replied to Bolan's warning with a nod. The Executioner released his seat belt, swiveling around to crank down his window. The rush of wind was nearly deafening. He couldn't hear the gunfire from the nearest chase car, swept away by velocity and baffled by serpentine curves, but he registered the hits with crystal clarity.

They'd been lucky so far, random hits on nonessential bodywork, but luck could only last so long. A few more moments, give or take. It only took one well-placed round to send them screaming off the road and into empty space.

He blanked the image out of his mind and concentrated on a means of shaking off the tight pursuit.

"Hang tough," he said to Monica. "I need to take the window out."

"All right."

It took the best part of a magazine to do the job, Lenart cringing under the shower of cartridge casings and pebbled safety glass as Bolan fired his MP-5K straight across the empty seat in back. When he cleared the window, he possessed a clear shot at their enemies, no risk of a precision burst deflected by obstructing glass.

"We need the inside track," he told her.

"Right."

Monica had been weaving back and forth across both lanes to keep their enemies from passing, every heartbeat spent in grim anticipation of another vehicle's appearance on the narrow track. A head-on crash would finish them, and it would be small consolation that their nearest adversaries would most likely blunder into the collision, rolling up too fast to use their brakes.

The warrior had another kind of ending for the chase in mind, and it didn't involve a fiery death for Monica, himself or the defector in their care.

But it would still take timing, angles, planning.

Luck, damn right.

On Bolan's order Monica slid over to the other lane, oblivious to danger now. She knew her companion's ploy would either work or it wouldn't, but either way it wouldn't take much time.

He saw the chase car make its move, a surge to pass, the driver grinning to himself behind the windshield. On the left-hand side both gunners had their windows down, prepared to fire the moment they were sure of scoring flesh. Another heartbeat. Just one more...

He fired for effect, a string of parabellum manglers blowing out the windshield and killing the driver where he sat. Beside him, in the shotgun seat, the gunner tried to scream and fire all at once. It was too late for either as his face exploded into crimson froth that spattered his two comrades in the back.

With dead hands on the wheel the chase car swerved and nosed in against the rocky mountainside with force enough to pitch the back-seat gunners forward. One of them exploded through the shattered windshield, sprawling on the hood, and Bolan registered a horrified expression on the guy's face. Then the second car came in with screeching brakes and struck the first one broadside, doing fifty miles per hour easily.

The shock of the explosion seemed to push them faster down the highway, riding on a gust of superheated air. From his position in the speeding rental car Bolan saw the chase cars merge as one, enveloped by a roiling ball of yellow flame before the twisted, flaming hulk rebounded to the edge and went over.

"My God," Monica gasped. "You did it. They're all gone!"

The Executioner picked up a glint of early-morning light on polished chrome, a third car coming down the mountain, maybe half a mile behind.

"Not yet."

18

Monica saw the fireball devour their enemies, sweeping them away, but her momentary surge of exhilaration was short-lived. She heard Belasko's cautionary words and checked the mirror, slowing just enough to let another car come into view.

More gunmen!

There could be no question of coincidence, given the circumstances. Any innocent motorist would have pulled over and stopped when he saw the explosion, but this one came on, weaving through the scattered debris and picking up speed again once he cleared the site of the blast. At least three men were inside the car, and while she couldn't see their faces Monica imagined the expressions they were wearing.

Some surprise, perhaps, that the initial ploy had failed. Determination to succeed. A lust for blood.

She couldn't see the town of Geiranger yet, but they were getting closer by the minute, hurtling downhill, with rubber crying on the curves. Beside her Belasko was keeping a steady eye—and gun—on their pursuers, while Lenart remained below the line of fire and hugged the floor.

She wondered how much longer they could last. And if they reached Geiranger...then, what? They'd still be forced to wait until the ferry made its scheduled run, and in the meantime they'd all be sitting ducks.

They were traveling along the Eagle Road, a zigzag course that would have thrilled her under any other circumstances with its waterfalls and panoramic vistas of the Hjelledal valley. At the moment, though, her mind was focused on the road ahead.

She checked her mirror, saw the chase car had reduced its lead a fraction and gave another nudge to the accelerator. Not too much, or she'd do the killers' job before they ever had a chance. She didn't relish the idea of driving off the highway, plummeting through space for several thousand feet and smashing on the jagged rocks below.

She risked a glance at Belasko and found him kneeling in his seat, facing backward toward the chase car and following its movements with his compact sub machine gun.

"How much farther?" he demanded.

They were getting close now. She could glimpse Geiranger below them as they rounded certain curves. There was an old church on the outskirts of the town, its steeple rising like a giant finger pointed toward the sky. If it had been a Sunday, they could easily have heard the bells from here.

"Perhaps a mile," she answered, flicking one last glance at their pursuers, bringing her full attention back to the treacherous roadway.

She could almost hear Belasko thinking to himself. The circumstances dictated tactics, and their enemies would have to make another effort very soon unless they planned on fighting through the streets of Geiranger. Even now it would be close enough for gunshots to be audible within the town, attracting notice, but if they could score a lucky hit within the next half mile or so...

Good luck for them, she thought. Bad luck for us.

She had the Walther automatic wedged beneath her right leg, close at hand, but she would never have an opportunity to use it now. Whatever happened in the next few moments, all that she could do was concentrate on driving to the best of her ability while Belasko tried to deal with their opponents.

"Watch yourself."

At first she thought the words were meant for her, but then she understood that he was speaking to Lenart. Belasko wormed his way between the separate seats in front, avoiding stepping on Lenart as best he could, and huddled on the back seat, that much closer to their enemies.

"Be ready." He directed the remark to Monica this time. "I need a slow-down on command, but nothing drastic. Just enough to give this crew some confidence."

"All right."

"Beginning...now!"

They swept around another curve, Monica applying gentle pressure to the brakes, fighting gravity all the way. She lost sight of their adversaries for a moment as the mountain intervened, but they were back again a heartbeat later.

Gunfire would be coming any second now, and it would only take one bullet punching through her seat or shattering her skull to send them off the road. There were so many things she still wanted to accomplish in her life, but at the moment one of them stood out.

She wanted to confront her contact, "Mr. Ragland," with the fact that he'd blown her cover, done his best to have her killed. She wanted to observe his face as he denied the charges . . . or if he admitted they were true.

There would be some excuse, of course, all neatly filed away and classified. Too bad. The need-to-know stopped here, and she would have the truth regardless.

If she only lived that long.

"DON'T MISS, for God's sake!"

In the circumstances no one caught the irony of Rostov's words, a die-hard atheistic Communist invoking God to help him kill. It was an admonition to the troops and nothing more.

"I can't hit anything unless you keep the damn car still!" Thadden snapped, leaning out the window with his machine pistol braced in a one-handed grip.

"It's not the car," Rostov snarled. "It's the road!"

For just an instant, after the explosion, he'd dared to hope his troubles might be over. Fire and wreckage had clogged the mountain highway, sliding, twisting with the sheer momentum of the crash, inexorably moving toward the brink . . . and gone. It had taken another curve, another look, for Rostov to discover that Lenart and company were still alive, still rolling on toward Geiranger, while Norner and his fried disciples hurtled down the cliff like shooting stars.

Incompetents.

It was a sorry comment on the state of terrorism in the world today that they'd been the best available to Rostov in a pinch. Not even true professionals, although they charged outlandish fees for planting bombs and shooting diplomats. At least he had to give them credit for the flair they had displayed in typing out communiqués.

All gone.

It was down to Rostov and his associates to finish off the game. They were perhaps ten minutes out of Geiranger, but they'd have to go ahead regardless of the risk from witnesses. The car was rented if it came to that, the contract name an alias, and any vague descriptions would be useless to police.

It seemed that Thadden was about to fire when someone in the lead car beat him to it. Rostov saw the muzzle-flash and wrenched the wheel to spoil the gunner's aim, afraid of overcompensating with a nosedive off the mountainside. It was a near thing even so, three bullets punching holes in the hood of the Mercedes, while a fourth round chipped the upper right-hand corner of the windshield.

Damn!

"The bastard's not half bad," Thadden said grudgingly. "That's how he dealt with Norner and the rest."

"You deal with him!" the Russian snapped, uncomfortable with the angry edge that had crept into his voice. He didn't like the feeling that he was about to lose control.

They roared around the next curve, trailing, when the lead car seemed to lose momentum, its brake lights flaring when the driver should have logically accelerated. Rostov saw the danger and tapped his own brakes hard enough to slow them down without a skid, and Thadden's burst of automatic fire was wasted on the rocks.

"Look out!"

Another raking burst erupted from the lead car, putting two more holes in Rostov's windshield, and he heard one of the headlights blow. No steam spouted from the radiator yet, and that was fortunate. To lose the engine now would be disastrous, leaving them on foot or forcing them to coast downhill with minimal control, the lifeless power steering more a hazard than a help.

Svoboda, in the back, was craning forward, staring through the windshield with its spiderweb of cracks and breathing heavily down Rostov's neck. He hadn't fired a shot so far, and there was no likelihood that he would. A useless piece of baggage.

"The only way to kill them is to get in closer," Thadden challenged, squeezing off an almost-wasted burst that added one ding to the lead car's pock-marked trunk. "Failing that, we have to ram them, force them off the road."

"We can't do that!" Svoboda blurted, clearly terrified. "My God, you'll kill us all. You saw what happened with—"

"Shut up!"

The Russian needed time to think, no matter if that time was measured in microseconds. Almost any risk was worth it to prevent a running battle through the streets of Geiranger, and he was prepared for a no-limit game, calling any bets the enemy cared to make.

It wasn't the defector, insignificant Gustave Lenart, that drove him on. Astrophysicists were a ruble a dozen in the Soviet Union, with more trooping out of the universities every day. The problem here—the only problem, as far as Alexandrei Rostov was concerned—involved the knowledge his enemies possessed.

If they could link the Einsatzgruppe to the KGB or any of its Eastern Bloc affiliates, however tenuously, then the plan for sabotaging *perestroika* would be blown sky-high. He had to kill the woman and her various accomplices before they found a friendly ear and spilled their stories. Otherwise...

He wouldn't think of the alternatives. They were too grim, and he had need of all his faculties at the moment, concentrating on the play at hand. The next few moments would decide.

"You're ready?"

Thadden didn't bother with an answer, both arms out the window now, his broad, blunt face gone nearly crimson from the rushing wind. This time when he fired the chunky German didn't mean to miss.

The lead car swept around another curve, momentarily lost to sight, and Rostov followed, understanding the thousand things that could go wrong—an engine stall, a flat tire, anything—to finish them. He felt as if his very force of will could keep the Mercedes rolling in pursuit of those he was determined to destroy.

If Alexandrei Rostov had believed in God or fate, he might have said it was his destiny. Instead, he simply saw a job unfinished, waiting to be done.

The technicality of murder never even crossed his mind. Lenart and company were traitors to the people's revolution and deserved to die for that alone, if nothing else.

For jeopardizing Rostov's master plan, they all deserved to rot in hell. And he would send them on their way to that reward within the next few moments.

BOLAN FIRED another short burst toward the chase car, more to slow it down than for effect. The hostile gunner answered with a wild burst of his own, and two rounds slapped the window frame a foot from Bolan's head.

One more like that and he might not have the time or opportunity to take them out. It was a lucky break, the two-for-one he had accomplished with the gunners from the Einsatzgruppe, but they were running short of time and tricks.

His adversaries might not mind a shoot-out in the streets of Geiranger below, but Bolan's private code had always called for minimizing the involvement of civilians in his private war. If there was any way to stop the final carload of assassins short before they reached the town, he had to try.

"How far?" he asked again.

"About a half mile."

He risked a glance across his shoulder through the windshield just in time to glimpse the church spire looming larger in the foreground. There were two or three more curves before they reached the classic landmark and descended into Geiranger itself.

No more time to waste then.

Bolan triggered off another burst, hardly aiming, before he reached back for one of the grenades, a little something extra that his enemies wouldn't expect.

It would require split-second timing for the optimum results. Disabling the chase car wouldn't be enough if any of the occupants were still alive. He had no wish to spend the next few days anticipating further confrontations, bracing to take a silenced round between the shoulder blades each time he went outside.

He wondered briefly who the gunners were, deciding that it hardly mattered. Einsatzgruppe survivors or some other faction with an interest in the game, they had the same effect. It had to be a clean sweep, all or nothing, for Lenart's as well as Bolan's peace of mind.

He palmed a fragmentation grenade and looped his thumb inside the safety ring. Five seconds on the fuse, and he would have to make the pitch precisely, with allowance for the chase car's forward motion. If the charge fell short or overshot his mark, if Bolan telegraphed his move and warned the enemy, it all would be in vain and he might not be given a second chance.

"We're almost there," Monica said. "I make it two more curves."

Behind them one of their assailants fired a burst that raked the rental car's flank and took out the taillights. A trifle lower and he could have hit the tires, a sure kill in the present circumstances.

Bolan couldn't wait to try his ploy, if it had any chance at all of working out.

He yanked the grenade's pin and let it drop into the seat beside him, holding the safety spoon firmly in place to avert premature detonation. He was counting down the seconds now, calculating distance, odds and angles for the pitch.

"Speed up a little if you can," he told Monica.

"Okay."

The rental car gave a forward surge, momentarily increasing the gap between the vehicles, but their shadow was determined to keep pace. Bolan took advantage of the fleeting lag, reached across the car's trunk and let go of the frag grenade.

It bounced once off the pockmarked trunk lid and was airborne, dropping out of sight before their progress showed it to him, spinning on the pavement like a top. Three seconds, four, and now the chase car was approaching, bearing down immediately on their track.

The blast was muted by their speed, the sound of rushing wind through open windows, but it did its job. The chase car's steering was disabled by a blast of shrapnel slicing cables, shredding rubber, and the driver lost control going into the last curve before Geiranger. The rental car was past it, sweeping downslope, when he saw their pursuers take flight, a snarling rocket that collided with the giant steeple, plunged through shingles, timbers, underpinning . . . And then an explosion and a churning ball of flame. The steeple roof was instantly involved as the concussion of the blast set off the church bells, pealing an alarm.

"Strike three," Bolan said, slumping in his seat beside Lenart. "I'd say they're out."

"And now?"

"We ditch the wheels and hardware and catch the ferry as planned. A sea cruise, anyone?"

EPILOGUE

George Cartland left his office at the U.S. Embassy in Oslo at five o'clock precisely, walking north at an easy pace. He had a leather briefcase in his hand and an umbrella tucked beneath his other arm. His bland face gave no indication whatsoever of the turmoil brewing in his mind.

How swiftly things disintegrated when they started going wrong. Two days, and he'd shifted from a mood of cautious optimism to a black depression unrelieved by alcohol.

So much bad news at once, and what was he to do with any of it now?

The Einsatzgruppe fiasco had been bad enough, still salvageable even when they missed the king in Lillehammer, but the latest news was nothing short of catastrophic.

The crash and fire would help, of course, and Rostov's men had been professionals. If they were carrying ID, it would be false, perhaps impossible to trace. And even if the mangled bodies *were* identified, there would be nothing to connect them with the embassy or Cartland's office. He was free and clear in that regard unless...

The woman.

She was still alive, and her behavior in the past two days showed clearly that she was aware of his duplicity. She had only to make one phone call, drop a letter in the mail and he was finished. Ruined. There was every likelihood that he would have to stand trial.

The answer that came readily to mind was an extension of his dealings with the KGB. He still had contacts in the city, one or two of whom might take on dirty work if they were well and promptly paid. Of course, he had to find the woman first before she made delivery on Lenart, so that her death would seem to be a consequence of the defection gone awry.

That done...

"Good evening, Mr. Ragland."

Startled by the voice behind him, Cartland turned and found himself confronted with the woman. She was staring at him with a cold look in her eyes, as good as telling him that she couldn't be bribed or pressured into backing down.

She meant to see him crucified.

Cartland rarely traveled armed, but he had been making an exception since this business with the Einsatzgruppe and Rostov. You could never be too careful in the field when you were flirting with the enemy. He was intensely conscious of the lightweight automatic pistol riding on his hip. It was a simple move to sweep his jacket back and draw the weapon, aim and fire at point-blank range.

"Thank heaven you're all right," he told her, stalling. "Christ, it's been two days without a word!"

"I'm fine, no thanks to you."

"What's that supposed to mean?" he asked, still bluffing, waiting for the perfect moment.

"I'll explain it at your hearing," Monica informed him, keeping up the cold front for effect.

"You're overwrought. If there's a problem, I can easily explain—"

"Not this time."

"Oh?"

"I'm filing formal charges. As it happens, they're already in the mail."

"That was a stupid thing to do. You could have saved yourself the trouble."

"But it's not my trouble anymore," she said. "It's yours."

"You think so?" He tried not to panic as he set the briefcase down and braced himself to draw the gun.

"I'd bet my life."

"You have."

It was a textbook draw, the way they taught it when he was still in training with the Company. Some things came back to you when you were under stress.

And it was almost good enough.

Almost.

The woman didn't have to draw. Her first round ripped through the handbag that she held, smashing into Cartland's chest below the sternum and slamming him against the nearby wall. The second shot was higher, dead on target, and it did the job.

George Cartland was dead before he hit the sidewalk in a sitting posture, braced against the wall, his woolen trousers soaking up the blood that pooled around his legs.

Across the street Mack Bolan waited in the car, the engine running. Monica slid in beside him, breathing hard, her eyes half-closed.

"He didn't leave me any choice," she said.

"I saw."

"It wasn't murder...was it?"

"No. The man passed judgment on himself. The reckoning was overdue."

"You make it sound so cold."

"That's how it is. If you hadn't taken him, I would have."

"So."

They drove in silence for the next few moments, putting the embassy behind them, pausing once to ditch Monica's automatic in an open sewer grate. Their path was winding toward the airport, but they still had ample time.

"You're going back today?" Bolan asked.

"Yes. There are a lot of questions I'll have to answer."

"If you need some help..."

She smiled and shook her head. "I'll do this on my own."

And do just fine, he thought, but kept it to himself. It would have sounded empty at the moment, and the lady deserved better than clichés.

"You staying with the Company?"

"I haven't decided yet. It depends on how things go...when I get back. And you?"

"The same," he told her after some reflection. "More of the same."

In the Deathlands, the only
thing that gets easier is dying.

JAMES AXLER

DEATH LANDS

Moon Fate

Out of the ruins of nuclear-torn America emerges a band of warrior-
survivalists, led by a one-eyed man called Ryan Cawdor. In their quest
to find a better life, they embark on a perilous odyssey across the rav-
aged wasteland known as Deathlands.

An ambush by a roving group of mutant Stickies puts Ryan in the clutches
of a tyrant who plans a human sacrifice as a symbol of his power. With
the rise of the new moon, Ryan Cawdor must meet his fate or chance
an escape through a deadly maze of uncharted canyons.

GOLD
EAGLE ®

DL16